WATERSHED

Other Books by
PERCIVAL EVERETT

Erasure
Grand Canyon, Inc.
Glyph
Frenzy
The Body of Martin Aguilera
God's Country
Big Picture
For Her Dark Skin
Zulus
The Weather and Women Treat Me Fair
Cutting Lisa
Walk Me to the Distance
Suder
The One That Got Away

WATERSHED

PERCIVAL EVERETT

For Kristen,
In friendship,

Beacon Press
Boston

Beacon Press
25 Beacon Street
Boston, Massachusetts 02108-2892
www.beacon.org

Beacon Press books are published under the auspices of the Unitarian
Universalist Association of Congregations.

07 06 05 04 03   8 7 6 5 4 3 2 1

This book is printed on acid-free paper that meets the uncoated paper
ANSI/NISO specifications for permanence as revised in 1992.

Library of Congress Cataloging-in-Publication Data
Everett, Percival L.
Watershed / Percival Everett. — 1st Beacon Press ed.
       p.   cm.
ISBN 0-8070-8361-5 (acid-free paper)
1. Indians of North America—Treaties—Fiction. 2. African American
men—Fiction. 3. Water rights—Fiction. 4. Hydrologists—Fiction. 5.
Colorado—Fiction. I. Title.
PS3555.V34W36 2003
813´.54 dc21
2003003619

For Chessie
As always, with love

Introduction

I used to believe that only Native American writers should write about Native Americans.

Since we Native Americans are so lacking in political, social, cultural, and economic power, since we are so voiceless, or are allowed only to speak at low volumes for small crowds, I believe that we are all too easily ignored. And when it comes to literature, Native American writers are most especially ignored. Of course, a few of us enjoy flourishing literary careers and a certain degree of mainstream success. But if we added up the sales figures of Louise Erdrich, Susan Power, Joy Harjo, Simon Ortiz, Greg Sarris, N. Scott Momaday, and all of the other publishing Native writers, including myself, I would guess that we, as an entire group, have sold fewer copies than Tony Hillerman, a non-Native who writes Navajo-based murder mysteries. I wouldn't be surprised if only one of Hillerman's best-sellers might have outsold all of us Indian writers put together. In a capitalistic country, money talks, and Hillerman's books certainly do a lot of shouting.

Am I jealous of Hillerman's success? Well, yes, of course, I am. I'd love to sell that many copies and enjoy that sort of mainstream success. But it's impossible for me to do so because I'm Native American, so by very definition, I can never be part of the mainstream, and neither can any other Native writer. As a result, we are excluded from any mainstream discussion about Native American lives. We live as Native Americans but we don't have any authority to speak as Native Americans.

Of course, there exists a greater paradox here. The entire

world is hungry for Native American stories. Hundreds of books are published each year about Native Americans. Hundreds of thousands of copies of those books are sold each year. So if this audience for Native American stories exists in such huge numbers, then why do Native American writers continue to be ignored? It's because the audience is hungry for a certain kind of Native American story, the stereotypical tales filled with wise elders, spiritual quests, half-naked warriors, noble political activists, and pantheistic philosophies. Thus, the most successful books are those that speak directly about Native American spirituality, or those books that incorporate Native American spirituality into a familiar genre like the murder mystery, romance novel, western, or period epic. Most importantly, for any particular book to appeal to mainstream tastes, it must also be nonthreatening to mainstream politics and culture. In the late nineteenth century, the U.S. government was terrified by the revolutionary nature of the Ghost Dance, an apocalyptic mishmash of Native cultural desperation and Christian righteousness, and slaughtered thousands because of that fear. But white leaders today are not afraid of Indian shamans, or non-Indians posing as shamans. Indian drunks, Indian dancers, and Indian mascots do not threaten white folks, either. When Indians are depicted and behave in familiar ways, they present no threat to any established belief system. Tony Hillerman's Navajo murder mysteries are so popular because they're well written and exciting, but equally important, because they do not challenge any mainstream notions about Navajo Indians in particular or Native Americans in general.

However, when Indians are depicted or behave in eccentric and unpredictable ways, they are highly threatening to non-Indians and non-Indian culture. I would venture that the most terrifying and powerful Indian in this country would be a single mother with a law degree. When I first realized that original aboriginals are scary monsters, I also understood that original Native writers are just as scary. A lack of mainstream success is not a curse for Native writers. Rather, I saw it as a sign of artistic and political courage, so I came to amend my beliefs about non-Natives writing about Native Americans.

I believe that non-Natives can write anything they want about Native Americans, but they are writing a colonial literature that merely confirms existing ideas. In politics, economics, and culture, white people have always presumed to speak for Native Americans, to know us better than we know ourselves, to represent our interests, and to define us. Christopher Columbus was our first surrogate storyteller, James Fenimore Cooper was our most rugged and distant, and Tony Hillerman is just one of the latest. Of course, in world terms, colonial literature is nothing new, but the United States is rarely described as a colonial country, except in terms of white Americans' rebellion from white English rule. Even today, the most liberal and progressive white folks rarely speak of themselves as colonists of Native Americans, and non-Native writers of Native American stories would never refer to themselves as colonial writers. Why? Because the story of white Americans' epic triumph over colonial rule is a more flattering story than Native Americans' continuing losses to colonial rule. Because if you took pro-Native sentiment to its end game, if non-Native champions of Native rights were absolutely committed to the cause, then they would naturally leave the country and move back to their aboriginal homelands. Because we all find it easier to judge sin than to confess sin.

And now, into this morass of colonialism and its contradictions comes Percival Everett's *Watershed*, a wonderful political thriller, love story, murder mystery, and literary novel seasoned with interracial politics, parody, and comedy. In *Watershed*, Everett fictionalizes the 1970s political battles on the Lakota

Sioux's Pine Ridge Reservation in South Dakota, combines them with fictional and real events during the 1960s civil rights battles for African Americans, and sets it all on a contemporary and fictional Indian reservation where a Native American dwarf and an African-American hydrologist struggle to save themselves and the tribe from evil corporate bastards. That's one description of this highly original book, but it's an inadequate description. While writing this introduction, I searched the Internet, and found every description of this book to be inadequate. I found all discussions and descriptions of Percival Everett and all of his books to be inadequate, and frankly, it pissed me off.

Here is a man, an African-American man, a Black man, a college professor, a novelist writing some of the most original work I've ever read, and he is so widely misunderstood and so widely ignored. I didn't find his work on college syllabuses or on required reading lists. I can't find his novels excerpted in the multicultural anthologies. I never read his name listed among the great African-American and American writers of our time. His many books have been published by a series of houses, rather than by one committed editor, and many of his works have fallen out of print. In short, everybody, including other African-American writers and scholars, is ignoring him. And I think Everett is being ignored precisely because he is so threatening.

In *Watershed*, Percival Everett portrays African-American and Native American characters that are startlingly original and eccentric. They are political activists who treat their loved ones terribly. They are tragic figures who are so funny. They are arrogant bastards who make incredible sacrifices. They are misogynists who defend the rights of women. They are civil rights fighters who are racist. They smoke cigarettes and drink booze while they complain about the evil nature of corporate capitalism. They are emotional stoics who yell and scream at a moment's notice. They are introspective dreamers who are blind to the needs of others. They are contradictory and complicated. They are sacred and profane. They are ugly, horrible, magical, and beautiful human beings. These people confused and frightened me. They angered and frustrated me. Just as I wish the real world was a better place to live, and real people were better than they are, and I a better man than I am, I constantly wished the characters in this book would finally, once and for all, make the right decisions and be good and pure and decent. But nothing happens that easy, and Percival Everett's *Watershed* is not an easy read.

I think the most difficult part about the book, the most dangerous idea it contains, is about the ambivalent nature of political activism. People can choose to die for their politics, of course, but they can also choose to kill for their politics. And, most tellingly in *Watershed*, political activists can also sacrifice the security of their families and friends, and the love of their children, in order to pursue indefinite ideas about justice. Whenever I read the news about the death of a freedom fighter, of a civil rights activist, I wonder if that martyred man or woman had children. When I read about the murders of American liberals fighting for children in far-off countries, I wonder if they left their own children at home. Why do we admire the liberal radical who leaves his family to fight for freedom, but denigrate the conservative businessman who leaves his family to make money?

Percival Everett understands that every individual human is morally ambivalent, that every human action has negative and positive reactions. Everett knows that the worst of us and the best of us are only separated by the thinnest of moral margins. And of course, that threatens not only white folks, but Black and Indian folks, as well. We brown-skinned folks want our real and fictional heroes to be clean and pure and unambiguous. We brown-skinned folks want our protagonists to redeem us. After centuries of oppression and ridicule, we brown-skinned folks want to be flattered and loved, not challenged and examined.

In all of his work, Everett challenges and examines us. In *Watershed*, he challenges and examines Native Americans in particular, and I, for one, think he is so original and so perceptive while doing so that he confounds all of my definitions about what is and what is not colonial literature. Can an African American, the descendant of slaves, ever be called a colonist? Can an African American write colonial literature? And considering the history of intermarriage between African and Native Americans, isn't it quite possible that Percival Everett has an Indian grandmother, and how does that change the meaning of this book? If a non-Indian Black can write a great book about Indians, can a non-Indian white write a great book about Indians? Well, of course, they can; white people have written many great books about Indians, so doesn't that make me a self-deluded liar? Does the quality of the art supercede all other political, economic, and social considerations? Should I care about the identity of the people who write great and challenging books about Indians? Or should I only hope that more great books about Indians are written and who gives a damn about the color of the author? Inside and outside of this book, Percival Everett interrogates me. He makes me doubt my most closely held beliefs and forces me to look at the world in new ways, and damn it, at the very heart of it, isn't that exactly what we want our very best writers to do?

Sherman Alexie

LANDSCAPES EVOLVE SEQUENTIALLY

*except under extraordinary provocation, or in circumstances not at all
to be apprehended, it is not probable that as many as five hundred
Indian warriors will ever again be mustered at one point for a fight;
and with the conflicting interests of the different tribes, and the occupation of the intervening country by advancing settlements, such an event
as a general Indian war can never occur in the United States. (Edward
Parmelee Smith, 1873)*

. . .

My blood is my own and my name is Robert Hawks. I am sitting
on a painted green wooden bench in a small Episcopal church on
the northern edge of the Plata Indian Reservation, holding in my
hands a Vietnam-era M-16, the butt of the weapon flat against the
plank floor between my feet. There are seven other armed people
sitting on the floor, backs against the paneled walls, or pacing and
peering out the windows—stained and clear—at the armored personnel carrier some hundred yards away across the dirt and gravel
parking lot, and at the pasture where two sad-looking bulls stand,
their sides, black and gray, flat against the sky behind them. Out
there, there are two hundred and fifty police—FBI, all clad in blue
windbreakers with large gold letters, and National Guardsmen,
looking like the soldiers they want to be. There is an FBI agent sitting in a chair opposite me; his hands are bound with yellow
nylon cord; his mouth is ungagged; his feet are bare and rubbing

against each other in this cold room. The hard look he had worn just hours ago has faded and, although his blue eyes show no fear, the continual licking of his lips betrays him. His partner, a shorter, wider man, is face down on the ground outside; his blood and last heat having melted the snow beneath him. He lies dead between two dead Indians, brothers, twins.

That I should feel put out or annoyed or even dismayed at having to tell this story is absurd since I do want the story told and since I am the only one who can properly and accurately reproduce it. There is no one else in whom I place sufficient trust to attempt a fair representation of the events—not that the events related would be anything less than factual, but that those chosen for exhibition would not cover the canvas with the stain or underpainting of truth—and of course truth necessarily exists only as perception and its subsequent recitation alters it. But I can tell it, my own incriminations aside.

· · ·

The insignificant point of light on the ceiling seemed to dilate as I watched, and I wondered how it was that the perforation would not let in enough light to illuminate even a section of the poorly lit room, but could allow in enough water to ruin the entire house; how it had to be in some way dark to see the distending prick, but water would always find me in there. I slapped myself for pondering like an idiot and did the only thing that made any sense: I grabbed my vest, the box of flies I'd tied the previous night, and my sixty-year-old Wright and McGill bamboo rod that no one could believe I actually got wet, much less used, and went fishing.

· · ·

Nymphs are meant to be fished near or on the bottom of the water and so must absorb moisture and/or be weighted so they get to the bottom quickly. The materials of their construction must give the appearance of life, suggesting the movement of a living insect in its larval or nymphal stage, its pulsing, vibrating. The fish get close to it, without the concern of the surface predators, and take a good look, and so it must be lifelike.

.   .   .

My father had never liked fishing. It seemed enough to him that my grandfather, his father, hunted and fished. My grandfather never pushed the idea on him, however. In fact, he confided in me that he understood my father needed the difference between them as a necessary point of divergence. "We're so much alike," he would say, then make a cast or load his rifle or rip the guts out of a fish in one quick motion. Indeed, he and my father looked enough alike to be brothers and to my mind, in matters all but those having to do with the outdoors, they shared the same beliefs. They were both physicians and both well liked, though to hear them speak you'd have assumed they found people objectionable and you would have been right, but it was people, not persons, who were problematic, they would articulately point out. They hated America, policemen, and especially churches. Their outright detestation for Christianity—it was much more than a simple disregard—had ended their marriages: my grandfather had known full well that his wife was a member of the AME Church but had hoped that he could live with it; my father claimed that my mother had found religion and bushwhacked him one day with a prayer at the dinner table. My grandmother died when I was ten and we went to the funeral, Christian service and all, and my aunt shouted at my grandfather, called him a heathen. She then turned to my father and said, "You're just as bad." She then knelt in front of me and tried to be nice, offering me a

Lifesaver—I said, "Blow it out your barracks bag." After my parents' divorce I lived with my mother, and the religious stuff weighed heavily on me, my being convinced that one had to be in some way born Christian because there was not a genuflecting bone in my body, and so my mother and I lived with our horns locked. The religious stuff became a lot more important than it should have been, as I did not actively dislike it, but simply did not care. When I was twelve, I went to live with my father and grandfather, whom "I was just like," and for four and a half years until I left for college, I watched the two of whom it would seem I was a pretty faithful copy.

. . .

The fishing turned out to be slow—I took three trout in a couple of hours, all on a store-bought Royal Coachman. I hated the generalized flies, the ones that didn't look like some particular insect native to the water but that because of their color or glitter caused the fish to strike them out of interest or anger or whatever, but I enjoyed following the green-and-red fly whiz through the air and light with its stark white calf-hair wings on the surface of the water. Anyway, the fish were small and I let them go. I switched to a hare's ear nymph and began to have pretty good success, starting on a string of keepers.

. . .

Before I came out here to the cabin, to fish and think and be alone, I was in the city with Karen, a woman I had been fucking. I decided on this term for our interaction, having found disfavor with the term *relationship* and seeing that I had simply and stupidly fallen into something out of convenience and, sadly, habit and, as with most things entered into easily, extricating myself turned out to be decidedly more difficult. Her voice grated on me, as did her attitudes and disposition, and finally her smells, but still I would lie between her legs again and again, pathetically seeking release or simply seeking.

"This is not a good time to go fishing," Karen had said, sitting at the kitchen table in my apartment, drumming her nails against the Formica, her index finger striking the place that had been chipped when I dropped my binoculars some months earlier. I just stood there, in sort of agreement, sort of nodding. We had been arguing, about what exactly was unclear now, but it had come, as it always did, to my defending myself by telling her that I did indeed care about her and that I did want to make her happy. As the discussion wore on I realized my lie and wanted to tell her that indeed I was not in love with her, never had been in love with her and, further, believed completely that she was too insane to be capable of love herself. Karen was a smart person and not unreasonable, but she wouldn't let me talk, wouldn't take a breath, and, sadly, as I was forced to listen now, was saying nothing new. "So, are you going fishing?" she had asked. Her drumming stopped.

Her words had sounded exactly like, "I dare you to go fishing." I studied her eyes and felt sick to my stomach at how I, in some way, genuinely detested her and her ways and here she was again daring me to do what I had done so many times before. I had been chanting in my head, and perhaps she heard it, that this was the last time, that this time I meant it, that there was no coming back, that I was turning the corner, no longer the weak man I had proven myself to be. I had said, "Yes."

"Why!?" she had screamed, her voice much louder than her size. "Because you need to get away from me? Am I that awful?"

"No, because I want to go fishing. I like fishing. It relaxes me."

"And I don't relax you?!"

. . .

That had been some weeks ago, just more than a month, when I had left Karen for the third and last time and come to the mountains. The weather was turning colder, with stiff winds from the northwest pressing through the canyons. I wondered if the fishing was relaxing me. It made the days pass and I was at least obliged to use my hands, for repairs on the cabin and tying flies — my hands needing the work, my eyes needing the attention to detail. And the fish didn't yell at me. They more often than not ignored me, but they didn't yell at me. I watched the no. 12 hare's ear I had tied the night before land and sink beneath the surface of the water.

. . .

Hook: Mustad 9674
Thread: Reddish or dark brown
Tail: Brown or ginger hackle fibers (1½ gap widths in length)
Rib: Fine gold tinsel
Abdomen: Hare's mask and ear dubbing fur blend
Wing case: Gray duck-wing quill section (folded over)
Thorax: Same as abdomen
Legs: Guard hairs plucked from under thorax with a dubbing needle

. . .

I had a string of six decent browns wrapped in newspaper. I took them down to the little store at the junction of the highway and the road off which I lived, hoping I could trade them for sundries.

"Hi, hon," Clara said as I walked in. She was a rough-looking woman with a soft, pleasant voice that came from beneath a massive mound of white hair and from behind oversized, red-framed bifocals. The glasses were new, one in a long line of pairs, as it seemed the woman was unable to locate her glasses once removed from her narrow face and set on some surface.

"Clara." I greeted her at the old brass-scrolled register she sat behind in the front of the store. Light found its way through the collecting clouds and into the store through the painted window beside her. "I brought you some trout. What do you say? Six fish for milk, butter, and eggs?"

"Why them ain't trout," she said, giving the fish a look, lifting her glasses and squinting, then gazing through both lenses of her bifocals. "Them's minnows."

"They told me they were trout."

"It's a deal then," Clara said, no smile, her lips tight. "But remember, I'm doing you a favor."

I felt the woman watching me as I collected the items from the refrigerator on the other side of the store, the air outside the unit fogging up the door as I held it open. I walked back toward her, smiling.

She said, as I dropped the butter on the counter with a thud, "You're pretty ugly for a young feller." She entered the routine smoothly, the same line as always; I assumed she reserved it for all younger men.

"Precocious."

"I call 'em likes I see 'em."

"A fine quality in anyone." I grabbed a loaf of rye bread from the unstable wire rack beside me and took some fruit, three bananas and ten apples, from the big wicker basket on the counter.

"How long do you think that many bananas are going to last you?" Clara asked.

"They get ripe too fast," I told her. "I like them while they're still a little green."

"Go figure ugly guys." She tallied in her head, her eyes disappearing behind the change in her lenses. "Let's call it two bucks."

I gave her the money.

"By the way, your lady friend called," Clara said, opening a paper sack with a snap and setting it on the counter. She looked at the message book she kept by the phone. "Let me see. She said call her back." My hands found the groceries and began to bag them. "You're welcome," she said. She watched me load the fruit into the bag. "So, you gonna call her?"

"What do you think I should do?"

"A feller what looks like you? I think you should call."

"You're probably right." I shook my head. "Still, I don't know. I don't know what to say. Suppose you were a woman, what would you want to hear me say?"

"That's why I like you," Clara laughed, then coughed, roughly. "Tell her to cut the crap and get the hell up here so you can frolic and cavort in the deep woods in your all-together. Either that or you go back down there where you can have anxious sex next to a banging radiator and traffic clatter outside the window."

"You do have a way of putting things." But, of course, I was not uncertain whether I should return the call. I felt the easiness of assured resolve, knowing and trusting, finally, my decision to abandon the sickness, as it were.

Clara nodded. "So what are you going to do?"

"I'm going to go home and fix the hole in my roof."

"What is that, some kind of metaphor?"

"Probably."

·   ·   ·

The Half-breeds of said tribes, and those persons, citizens of the United States who have intermarried with Indian women of said tribe and continue to maintain domestic relations with them, shall not be compelled to remove to said reservation, but shall be allowed to remain undisturbed upon the lands herein above ceded and relinquished to the United States.

·   ·   ·

Outside, I fell in behind the wheel of my pickup, turned the key, and heard the engine try but fail to start. I pumped the gas pedal and turned the key again. A third time. A fourth. I sighed and leaned forward to rest my head on the steering wheel. I didn't feel anxious or even put out; that was what the mountain did for me. So the car wouldn't start—the car could be fixed. It might take a little time, but time was free and it might take a little money, but money was just money.

"Pop the hood," a small voice said. I looked out the open window and saw no one, then glancing slightly downward I found a very short woman. The woman was the size of a child, with her dark hair pulled tightly back exposing a largish, almost hooked nose and oddly flat cheekbones. "Pop the hood," she said again.

"Doesn't need to be popped," I told her and watched her walk around to the front of my truck. I could see the top of her head as she searched for, then found and released the hood latch. Then I couldn't see her, but I heard her climbing onto the bumper as she pushed open the hood, heard her fumbling around on my engine. I stayed put and waited.

"Try it now," she called.

I turned the key and the truck fired up. The small woman walked around to the back of the truck. I watched in my mirror as she picked up a knapsack and stowed it in the bed just behind the cab. She opened the passenger-side door and climbed in beside me, scooting her butt back into the seat and fastening the belt. The shoulder strap bothered her face and so she put it under her arm.

"Thanks," I said to her. "I guess I do owe you a ride. Where am I taking you?"

"Just go wherever you were going."

"I live twenty-five miles up the road," I said, expecting that to give her pause.

"That's fine."

"You don't want to go to my house. And there's nothing else up there."

"No, just get me close to the lake."

I looked back over my shoulder into the bed at her pack, red with yellow pockets. She was diminutive, so her clothes were no doubt little, but still her pack seemed slight: no tent, no pad, no sleeping bag. "You don't have much gear," I said. "You know, it gets cold up there."

"Let's just go."

"So, what was wrong with my engine?" I asked, backing away from the planking of the store's porch and driving out onto the road.

"I don't know. I just jiggled a do-hickey."

"You'll have to show it to me. The do-hickey. In case that ever happens again." I glanced at her briefly. "It sounded like the distributor wire was loose." I looked at her again, but she kept her eyes straight ahead. "You know the old trick where you disable a car and then fix it so the person will give you a ride?"

"That's an old trick?" She didn't look at me.

"I've never heard of anybody doing it. Actually, I just thought it up."

"So what you're telling me is that you're paranoid."

"It doesn't sound good when you say it," I said.

The woman laughed. "My name is Louise."

"Robert." I shook her hand, her little bones feeling unreal in my grasp, feeling as though they might break, rolling together under my thumb the way I had once felt my mother's roll together when she was old. After another glance at her gear I asked, "Just planning a hike back down the trail?"

"Yes," Louise said quickly, too quickly, quickly enough to tell me to shut up, quickly enough to raise if not concern, then my curiosity.

I observed her canvas sneakers with their white, semicircled rubber toes, then looked at the slate sky. "You realize it's likely to snow today. I haven't heard the report, but it looks like snow."

Louise looked at the sky, leaning her small frame forward, her dark eyes searching.

"I mention it because of your shoes."

"Oh, I've got boots in my pack."

"I see."

I felt her uneasiness and so I backed off, attending to my driving, putting both hands on the wheel. I hoped that I had not made her feel that I was interested in her. I felt somewhat badly that her size, or lack thereof, had caused me to believe she was not quite capable of taking care of herself. It was a stupid thing to think, but I couldn't deny it, and I recognized and acknowledged once again one of my problems—my inability to deny conveniently some stupidity of mine, even momentarily. It seemed that, at every opportunity, I examined closely the nature, structure, and philosophical ramifications of my stupid feelings, a kind of over-the-top second-order thinking that turned out to be a detaching device rather than a constructive exercise.

I pulled off to the side of the road and stopped. "Well," I said, "my place is a couple of miles down this muffler-buster. The lake and trail head are just half a mile on. Would you like me to drive you the rest of the way?"

"No, that won't be necessary. Thanks for the ride." And she lifted the handle and pushed open the door and got out. She closed the door, went to the back of the truck, and leaned her body over the bed wall to retrieve her pack. She stepped away and waved to me.

I drove on down the lane, watching her grow even smaller in my mirror. She was still standing there when I rounded the bend and lost sight of her.

. . .

Plata Creek Indian Community v. United States, No. C.V.-99-3456-R (filed Dec. 22, 1984). The Indian Community seeks a federal review of its charges under the Administrative Procedure Act to the Secretary of the Interior's resolution to omit tribal lands from the Hellhole Creek Project. The Indian Community maintains that the project benefits only non-Indian residents of the area and that the Secretary has not complied with the 1916 federal act directing him to designate 768 twenty-acre plots and to provide for water rights to irrigate them in perpetuity.

. . .

I parked in front of my cabin, opened the truck door, and sat there staring up at the brown-shingled roof and the intimidating sky above it. I'd put off the patching job for some time, but I couldn't any longer. I went into the house, put the food away, and made a mental note to go through the shelves later to discard the spoiled stuff. Then I got the ladder from the shed and brought it into the house, knocking over, as I always did when carrying something into the house, the too-small cowboy hat I kept hanging on a nail by the door. I set the ladder where I had been sitting earlier, from where I had been able to detect the cancerous puncture; then I climbed the rungs, found the tiny hole between the boards, and pushed a broom straw through it. I next took the ladder outside where I used it to get on the roof. I found the straw and marked the spot with a scratch of white chalk. I stood and looked around and remembered how I didn't much care for roofs. Heights didn't bother me, but roofs—the pitches of roofs, the materials of roofs—did: especially metal roofs, which this one was not, but still the thought of it bothered me, the thought of the slick surface, of the sound of my steps on the tin, the jagged rips.

I cut some material from the roll of extra roofing felt that had been stored in the shed, grabbed a leftover shingle from the stack of several, and went out and climbed back onto the roof. The air turned frigid quickly, and when I looked at the sky I could see the snow coming: small flakes that seemed to disappear before they reached me at first, then crystals that kissed my neck and made me cold. I peeled back the shingles on the problem spot, glued down a patch of felt, and nailed down the new shingle to replace the old. It was not a great job, probably it wasn't even the correct way to do it, but it was done and I kicked myself for not having performed the simple task much sooner. The snow fell in larger flakes and began to stick to the rhododendrons against the wall of the shed. From my perch, I looked in the direction of the road, but could see nothing, just the gray of the bad weather closing in.

I climbed down, put away the ladder, and collected a load of wood from the pile I'd chopped earlier. I went into the house and dropped the fuel by the stove, then went back outside and secured the tarp over the stacked logs beside the house before taking in another lading of wood.

Inside, I fried some eggs and a trout with the head still on it, an eye staring up at me. I sat down to it, thinking all the while about that little woman Louise out there someplace in the cold without proper gear. It was her business though. I didn't care who froze to death from their own witlessness or considered deliberation.

.   .   .

When I was eight my grandfather took me hunting for wild turkey. Once out of the city he was alert to any human movement, saying that if the rednecks found you alone, there was no telling what might happen, or more to the point, it was far too predictable what would happen.

"What would you do if some KKKs grabbed your grandfather right now?" he asked as he knelt to observe some sign, his fingers moving over the ground that had been scratched up, feeling the freshness of a bird's excrement.

"I'd run for help," I said.

"To whom would you run?"

"The police," I said.

He nodded, then sat on the ground and looked at me. "When you're older," he said, "the police will stop you and search you and, if they don't shoot you, they'll take you in and say you look like another 'nigger.' They may not use that word, but that's what they'll mean. It's happened to me. It's happened to your father. It will happen to you."

"So, I shouldn't go to the police?"

He smiled at me. "Yes, you should go to the police. Where else can you go?"

. . .

Hell-hole Lake was established in 1907 with BIA funds which had been set aside for the Plata Creek Tribe. The Plata Creek Indian Community at that time sought [compensation], but was not allowed to sue the federal government for misappropriation of funds set aside for Indian use, because they were not considered a collective body until 1934 and the passage of the Indian Reorganization Act and because the Secretary of the Interior at that time, Joe Schmo, called the Indian challenges offensive because of their use of the word "theft."

. . .

It was almost dark outside and the book I was reading was putting me surely to sleep. The stove was stoked and just getting hot and the pull of sleep felt good. That's when a banging at the front door came, although it didn't cause me to bolt from my chair. Instead, I leaned forward and rubbed my face as I yawned. The banging came again and I got up and walked toward the door.

"Who is it?" I asked, sternly, hoping that if the knocker was trouble I might scare him away.

The knock was repeated, loud, but somehow thin.

At the door now, "Who is it?"

"Louise," the small voice said.

I opened up and she stepped by me into the house. I looked outside into the night and falling snow, shut the door, and locked it. I studied the woman for a few seconds. She was wet, soaking wet, her hair defeated about her narrow shoulders; her sneakers, ice-covered and darkened, were making puddles on the planks of my floor.

"You'd better get over there by the stove," I said. "Get those shoes and socks off before your toes freeze." She moved toward the heat. "And the rest of the wet things, too. I'll get you a robe." I went into the bedroom and came back with a pair of striped pajamas that had been a gift from Karen. I had worn them once and they had nearly strangled me to death in my sleep. "As it turns out, I don't have a robe," I said, "but you can put these on." Louise was stripped down to her underpants and bra. I turned away, having seen her little body, her small breasts, and her waist no bigger than my thigh.

"Thanks for letting me in," she said.

"You bet."

"Okay, you can turn around," she said.

I did and I saw her holding herself tightly, lost in the cotton pajama shirt that fell to her ankles. The bottoms were still folded on the chair beside her.

"Do you feel better?" I asked.

She nodded, showing her palms the heat of the stove.

"Are you crazy?" I asked. I opened the stove and poked at the logs to get the flame up, burning myself slightly on the inside edge of the door. "I didn't say anything in the truck because I thought it was none of my business. But now that you're in my house and wearing my clothes . . ." I paused while I closed the stove. "Another hour out there and you might be dead, or at least missing a few fingers and toes."

. . .

Before the action of deglutition, the pharynx is pulled upward and opened in a different direction; this is in order to receive the food thrown into it by the mouth. Once received into the pharynx, the elevator muscles relax and the constrictors contract upon the food and transport it down into the esophagus.

. . .

She didn't say anything.

"Listen, I'm going to make some tea." I felt badly for scolding her. I walked over to the kitchen and from the cupboard pulled down the old coffee can in which I kept tea bags. I took a couple of mugs from the rack, one bearing the name Canyon City, Colorado, and the other Wellfleet, Massachusetts. "So, what are you doing out here?" I asked, dropping the tea bags into the cups. Louise didn't answer, but she was now sitting in the chair in front of the stove, her tiny toes wiggling, obviously hurting her as feeling worked back into them. I walked back across the room with the mugs and poured water into them from the kettle I kept sitting on top of the stove. "It's a good sign that you can wiggle your toes like that."

She nodded.

"Do you take milk?" I asked.

"No."

"Would you like Canyon City or Wellfleet?" I asked, but she

said nothing. "I'll give you Wellfleet," I said, handing her the mug. "It's a little town on Cape Cod and it has one of my all-time favorite traffic signs. 'Thickly settled,' it says."

She thanked me for the tea and sipped it.

"Listen," I began again, "I don't want to belabor the point, but are you crazy?" I took her silence as an affirmative response. "I guess there's no more to say then. Tomorrow, I'll drive you back down to town and you can check into some dementia retreat."

"I can find my way."

"I can't let you go out there and become coyote feed."

Louise's face tightened. "If I were a six-foot man, you wouldn't be talking to me like this."

"Well, you're wrong. I might be a little more afraid of someone who was bigger and crazy, but I'd be saying the same thing to a six-foot idiot who was sitting in front of my fire, half-frozen, lost, in my pajamas, and saying he was going out into the snow and deep freeze in sneakers and a sweater." I drank some tea. "You can do whatever you want, but I just need to know, for myself, that I tried to discourage you. I'd offer you my boots and some clothes, but the problem is obvious." I looked at her face and saw that she was indeed listening. "All I have to offer you is my roof, my fire, and food. Tomorrow, you can do what you want."

"Thank you," she said, putting down her mug on the floor by her feet.

"Are you hungry?" I asked.

"No." She looked around the cabin and then at me. "What do you do?"

"I fish," I said. I looked down at the surface of my tea, at a piece of leaf floating there, and I poked at it with my finger.

"No, I mean for a living."

"I'm a hydrologist," I told her. I realized that she was shaking, but not with cold. She was scared.

We sat there for a while without talking.

"Do you have any socks I can use?" she asked. "My feet are getting cold or too hot or something."

"Yeah, I've got some socks."

.   .   .

During the field study, 23–27 September, examinations of the geology, hydrology, and soil-erosion processes were made of the Plata Mountain watershed. Observations of the Plata and Silly Man Creeks were made from Rural Route 13 above the confluence of the Silly Man and Red Creeks, from the mining road numbered A-28 traversing north-south along Silly Man Ridge and from various locations along the two main creeks.

The study revealed that at least four major plateaus make up the Plata Mountain watershed. The presence of these terraces, and observations of the deposition pattern within the terraces, indicate at least two, and perhaps more, periods of downcutting and aggradation. The oldest plateau consists of undercut banks and ridges and is more pronounced in the eastern portion of the watershed, facing west to the opening of Tick Canyon. Tick Canyon streams and flood events meet and cut into Plata Canyon, and join Plata Canyon and Creek. Traces of an older, alluvial terrace can be found at higher elevations within the adjoining canyons of Skinner, Dog, and, to a lesser extent, in Hell-hole watersheds, where there are apparent cycles of aggradation as well.

.   .   .

My grandmother baked pies. All the time. There were always pies. One day, it could have been any day, I was eating pie in her kitchen. I was less than ten, I remember. I must have been. I watched her pull another pie from the oven. Blueberry.

"You don't like Grandfather," I said.

"Your grandfather is a very smart man," she said.

"But you don't like him?"

"He's very smart."

.   .   .

We were in my truck driving down the twenty-five icy miles to Clara's store. "Why don't you let me drive you all the way to Plata?" I asked.

"The junction will be fine," she said and, when I didn't press, I felt her looking at me. "What kind of hydrologist?" she asked.

"The boring kind," I said. When I looked over at her I could see the answer wasn't amusing to her. "I've been studying the watershed of Plata Mountain for the Naturalists' Conservancy."

She nodded.

"It allows me to live here. I've studied the flow of the Plata and some of the creeks for Fish and Game as well."

"The mountain is dying," she said. "My grandfather told me that before he died. He said the river is no longer any good. He said the Plata can't feed the fish."

"The Plata is in trouble, but it's not dying."

"You should come to the reservation and meet my people. They're a part of this land. I didn't grow up here, so I'm not. But my mother is as much a part of this land as Silly Man Creek."

I nodded.

I could feel her looking at me. I could feel her thinking. "How can a river be in trouble and not be dying?" she asked.

I didn't have an answer for her.

"Our way tells us that when the river dies, so will our people."

I nodded again.

.   .   .

I let Louise out just above the store at the crossroads. As she closed the door, I asked, "What's your last name?"

"Yellow Calf," she said, and I could see that the information had been released automatically and that she was sorry for that. She closed the door and walked away along the main highway. I drove down to the store, parked, and went inside.

I was greeted with "Your girlfriend called again" from Clara. She was standing behind the counter, pulling red jelly beans from a many-colored pile of jelly beans on the surface in front of her. I watched her long liver-spotted fingers at work. "Why are you doing that?"

"I charge more for the red. People like the red ones, so I pull them out and charge more." She glanced up at my frown and shook her head. "Don't give me a hard time. You're willing to pay a few cents more for brown eggs." She passed a broken bean through her lips. "All eggs are the same," Clara said, popping another piece of candy into her mouth. "Why prefer the brown ones?"

I poured myself a cup of coffee. "Tell her to stop calling you," I said, changing the subject.

"What?"

"When she calls again, tell her to stop bothering you. Tell her to stop tying up your business line."

Clara nodded. "If you want me to, but I kinda think you ought to tell her yourself."

I looked at Clara and felt small. I put down my mug on the counter and said, "Let me have the phone." She set it down in front of me, right in the middle of all the jelly beans, and told me she thought I was doing the right thing. I told her to shut up.

I dialed Karen's number, it hurting me with each pressed tone that I knew her number by heart, and waited through a couple of rings. "Hello, Karen. This is Robert. I'm still up here fishing. I hope you're well. Please don't call me anymore." I hung up.

Clara watched the receiver go down into its cradle and then looked up at me. "I'm impressed."

"It was her answering machine."

Clara smirked.

"By the way, I like the orange ones."

.   .   .

Observed also were expansive structural relations in the region, including the Silly Man Ridge monocline, a fault running north-south, several east-west faults, and a portion of Plata Mountain. Another fault, which is suggested by the topographical features of the west face of Plata Mountain, may have some impact on surface drainage. The major north-south fault and the east-west structural facets in Plata Canyon have impacted the Plata Mountain watershed itself, evidenced in the field, and confirming Fran Rocker's work on the geology of Plata Mountain watershed (USGS Paper 45679-T [1981]).

.   .   .

When I arrived at the little store/gas station at the intersection of two highways that was Plata Township, the sun was just touching the tops of the mountains of the Crow Creek range, making them golden and ochre, cutting them sharply against the horizon. I went into the store and grabbed a package of Twinkies from the wooden shelf by the cash register. A couple of older men in cowboy hats were in line in front of me.

"My bull is sick," the wider of the two said. "He's got these black spots on his throat." He kept tucking his shirt into the back of his trousers with his free hand.

"Hmm," the second man said. "I bet it's screwworm."

"Have you ever seen this screwworm?"

"No, but I'll bet that's it. You should call the vet and have him come out and look. My cows, they got them spots and the vet field agent came out and that's what he said. Screwworm. He gave them some shots, but the spots, they are still there."

The men walked out and I stepped to the register.

"Health food nut, eh?" the young woman said, picking up the Twinkies to look at the price. "You check the date on these?"

"They never go bad."

"That it?"

I took a roll of wintergreen mints from the paper box by the till and let them roll across the counter.

"Ninety-eight cents."

I gave the woman a dollar.

"And you get two whole cents back," she said, smiling, a gold tooth midway back on the left side of her mouth showing.

"Do you know the Yellow Calf family?"

"I know where they live," she said.

A young man behind me who smelled of garlic and beer asked the woman for a pack of filterless Pall Mall cigarettes.

"Where can I find their house?" I asked.

The woman pointed out the store and toward the intersection where a suspended amber light flashed. "South, seven mailboxes, after the trailer what has no roof."

.   .   .

My father read to me when I was a child. What he read was Lewis Carroll's *Symbolic Logic*. He would read me a passage about existential statements, look at the expression on my face, and then laugh. I would laugh too and we would recite syllogisms together—if *a* then *b*, if *b* then *c*, therefore if *a* then *c*—and he would have me insert statements for *a*, *b*, and *c* until I was brain-tired and fell asleep. My father taught me to be a smart-ass and it became a thing I couldn't help; throughout my life I was said to have "an attitude." And so I did, I suppose. A crop of attitude planted by my father and encouraged by my grandfather.

In seventh grade I was asked by a science teacher, a Mr. Yount, who looked very much like his name, to tell the class what I thought venereal disease was. I said, "I believe it is a shaft infection."

2

I lost count of the mailboxes and though I spotted the topless trailer, it was the yellow-and-white paramedics' vehicle and the accompanying flashing red lights that led me to the Yellow Calf home. I thought to keep driving, but I saw Louise standing in the yard. She was the same height as several, obviously frightened, children. I parked on the road; my car was leaning severely as it was next to the drainage ditch. I had to push hard against the door to close it.

Louise turned and raised an awkward, absent wave. She seemed to take a second to recognize me, and having done so seemed conspicuously unimpressed.

"Can I help in some way?" I asked.

"It's my mother," Louise said, stoically. "She's old."

At that moment, the medics brought the old woman out onto the porch on a stretcher, her body held in place by red-and-yellow straps. She was in obvious pain, her head was rolling from side to side and her eyes were shut tightly, but she made no sound. The light of the day was fading and the flashing red lights of the ambulance seemed brighter, sweeping over a larger area. "It's okay, kids," Louise said to the children. A large man, a young obese woman, and an elderly woman came out of the house after the stretcher.

"Do you know what's wrong?" I asked, feeling stupid, not knowing really what to say, not knowing why I had actually stopped after seeing the ambulance.

"She's old. The pain is in her stomach." She stepped away from me and announced to the other adults, "I'm riding with Old Woman in the ambulance. Robert here will drive the rest of you." She turned to the children. "You run over to Irene's. Go straight there."

The children ran on.

The big man and the big woman sat in the bed of the truck, their backs to the cab, their heads in my view when I glanced at the mirror. The elderly woman sat in the cab with me.

"My name is Robert," I said, glancing at her and then through the windshield at the flashing lights of the ambulance that was disappearing ahead of us.

"My name is Mary Brown," she said without looking at me. "My brother's wife is ill."

.   .   .

I sat in an orange molded plastic chair that hurt my back in the waiting room of the Rivertown Hospital. The large man who had ridden in the back of my truck from the reservation was named Big Junior Brown, and he was now seated across the magazine-covered coffee table, sharing a bag of corn chips with his obese wife, Della. Della was missing the tip of her right index finger and she played constantly with the smooth end of it while she ate. I couldn't watch her because of that. Mary Brown was standing at the window and looking out at the parking lot two stories below. Louise was at the curved nurses' station, trying to get some piece of insurance business ironed out. I didn't know what to do with my hands, so I picked up a magazine and began to thumb through it.

"You're a friend of Louise?" Big Junior asked. He didn't have any teeth in the front of his mouth.

I nodded. "Actually, we just met the other day."

Big Junior tossed in another handful of chips. "What year is your truck?" I told him it was a '78 and he said he liked riding in the back of it and that he'd noticed that it was a four-by-four and asked me if I wanted to sell it. When I told him I didn't, he said, "It's a nice truck. Della likes it, too."

Louise came over and sat next to me, but she attended to the others. "They have to do some tests," she said. "They want to scope her and do a biopsy."

Mary Brown had turned from the window to listen to her niece's words, but they obviously meant nothing to her. "Does she have to stay here?" the old woman asked.

"For a while," Louise said.

Mary Brown looked at Della. "Tomorrow, you go by Georgie Head's and tell him I'll be coming by to see him."

Della nodded.

To Big Junior, Mary Brown said, "Go out to that little store and buy me a carton of cigarettes."

. . .

It is not uncommon for gallstones to cause intestinal obstructions (see Brockis and Gilbert: "Review of 179 Cases," British Journal of Surgery, 44:461, 1957 and Kirkland and Croce: "Gallstone Intestinal Obstruction," Journal of the American Medical Association, 176:494, 1961). However, the cause is often slowly recognized. The occurrence of gallstone ileus is nearly without exception due to binary-enteric fistula formation, the most usual locations of the fistula being the duodenum, colon, jejunum, and stomach. A case was reported where complicated cholecystitis with accompanying gastric obstruction appeared as carcinoma of the antrum of the stomach due to gallstones (Kavetz and Gilmore, "Cholecysto-Gastric Fistula Masquerading as Carcinoma of the Stomach," Annals of Surgery, 159:461, 1964).

. . .

"They think she might have cancer," Louise said. She drank from her steaming cup of coffee. There was a white-haired woman sitting in the booth behind Louise. The expanse of head and hair served to frame Louise's face with a bleached halo.

I caught a passing waitress. "Can we get some bread here, please?" To Louise, I said, "That's pretty tough."

Louise shrugged, rubbed at the corners of her eyes with a knuckle. "I was certainly surprised to see you tonight."

"Well, I'm sorry I picked such a bad time." Feeling ravenous, I eyed the packages of honey in a bowl by the napkin dispenser. "I haven't eaten today," I said.

"My mother's a tough bird," Louise said.

"I can imagine," I said. "If she had anything to do with raising you, she would have to be."

Louise laughed. "I'm sorry I gave you such a hard time the other night."

"That's all right, but I'd still like to know what you thought you were doing up there."

"I was just looking around." She peered across the room toward the closed salad bar. "I'm glad you did show up tonight though," she said as her little fingers ripped a napkin into strips.

"Why is that?"

"You turned out to be useful. I guess the polite way to put it would be 'helpful.' You know, driving Mary, Big Junior, and Della to the hospital. I want to thank you for that."

I nodded. "Would you like me to drive them back to the reservation?"

"No. Mary's going to stay at the hospital with me and Big Junior's brother is coming to get him and Della."

The waitress glided by and deposited a basket of cold bread on the table. I offered some to Louise first, and after she declined, I took a roll and bit into it. "I hate being hungry," I said.

"Coming here instead of staying at the hospital commissary was a good idea," Louise said. "That place is really depressing. I've spent too much time there recently."

"Cancer, eh?"

Louise looked at her pile of napkin tearings. "It would be no surprise, but it's not cancer."

"It's not? How do you know?"

"Hiram Kills Enemy told us last week. He came by and looked at my mother and said she should drink some tea made from the root of sweet flag."

"Did your mother do it?"

"No, she's afraid of Hiram. I mean, really afraid of him, says he fools around with powers, stuff like that."

I nodded. I didn't understand, but I nodded.

"You think this is weird shit," Louise said.

I nodded again.

. . .

The symptoms of Wanda Yellow Calf, an eighty-one-year-old Plata Indian woman, when admitted were progressive nausea, anorexia, weight loss, gastric pain, and postprandial vomiting. It was reported by the daughter that the pain was nonradiating, was increased when eating, and relieved by regurgitation. Although the symptoms had been observed in the home for a period of two to three weeks, this was the first medical visit. The patient was observed to have an enlarged nodular liver and a low-grade fever. Liver functions were observed as normal. It was reported by the family that the patient did not drink alcohol.

The serum cholesterol of the patient was 141 mg/100ml. Serum-glutamic-oxaloacetic-transaminase was 65 units/100ml. As well, urine specific gravity was 1.213 and 7–10 white blood cells per high-powered field were found. Blood urea nitrogen was 39.7 mg/100 ml when admitted and later 19 mg/100 ml.

Initial diagnostic speculation was carcinoma of the stomach with possible metastases to the liver. Because of retained secretions, upper gastrointestinal X rays were inconclusive. Following extended gastric suction, X rays disclosed a stenosing antral lesion. Interpretation of subsequent film substantiated the earlier conjecture of carcinoma.

. . .

I went home thinking it was all weird shit. It was about two in the morning and the cold sky was as clear as it could be. The stars were big. I thought about the name *Kills Enemy* and wished I had a name like that. I remembered the name of a man I saw in an old photograph once. His name was *Old Man Afraid of His Horses*. In the picture he stood next to the unfortunate man whose name was *Unidentified Indian*.

. . .

At the store a few days later, there because I'd ripped a hook through my finger and didn't have antibiotic cream at the cabin, I heard a couple of fellows talking. They talked about the "damn Indians" and one said they didn't need the "fuckin'" water "no way" and that they were just trying to be militant and get even with the "Great White Father."

I was leaning over in front of the shelf, trying to decide between a cream and an ointment.

Clara walked by me. "Hey, ugly."

I chose a product because I liked the color of the box and because it was the only antibiotic cream there. I walked to the counter to pay, grabbing a bag of chips along the way.

The two men by the door stopped talking. One of them looked at me, then said, "You're a hydrologist, right?" He didn't wait for a response and raked under his nose with the back of his hand, saying, "What do you think?"

"What do I think about what?" I asked.

"About the water. Whose water is it?"

"I just study water. I don't know whose it is."

"You gotta have an opinion," the other man said. He was truly ugly. His face was pocked with scars and his nose was bent to one side between bloodshot, pale blue eyes.

"I'm afraid I don't."

"But you gotta," the man said, stepping closer, and I could detect the slightest trace of alcohol in his breath. He made me nervous. He seemed mad and that confused me and then I got angry because I didn't like being confused like that.

"I don't 'gotta' have anything," I told him, looking at his tired, sick eyes.

"Them Injuns, they just want all the water for themselves," he said. "They're just fuckin' greedy."

"Well," I said, "what they want it for won't use it all up either. Seems to me there's a lot of water. Besides, the treaty says it's theirs. They were here first."

"See, I knew you had an opinion. You're on their side." He stepped closer to me.

"If I have to be on a side, I guess it won't be yours."

"I need that water."

"Pay them for it," I said.

"That's enough," Clara said.

Another man came running into the store, out of breath, leaning over to catch up with himself.

"What the hell is it, Dixon?" Clara asked him.

"They just found two FBI men dead up at the lake."

"No shit," the sick-eyed man said.

"Yeah," Dixon said. "The deputy, Hanson, found them. Shot to death. Both of them. Shot dead."

The three men left the store together, piled into one of their pickups as though they were important and needed to see the scene, and sped away up the mountain in the direction of the lake.

Clara whistled.

. . .

Article 3. The lands retained and to be held by the members of the Plata Indians, under and by virtue of the first article of this agreement, shall, to all intents and purposes whatever deemed and held to be an Indian reservation, and the laws which have been or may hereafter be enacted by Congress to regulate trade and intercourse with the Indian tribes, shall have full force and effect over and within the limits of the same; and no persons other than the members of said band, to be ascertained and defined under such regulations as the Secretary of the Interior shall prescribe (unless such as may be duly licensed to trade with said band, or employed for their benefit, or members of the family of such persons) shall be permitted to reside or make any settlement upon any part of said reservation; and the timbered land allotted to individuals, and also that reserved for subsequent distribution, as provided in the first article of this agreement, shall be free from all trespass, use, or occupation, except as hereinafter provided.

, .

The news of the murders spread through the valley. The radio buzzed crazily with it and everyone had a theory. A teenager called in to say he'd recently seen a spaceship and figured the agents were up the mountain making contact. A woman who claimed to be a geophysicist, but who wouldn't say where she lived, stated for a fact that the government was going to build another super-collider on the big mountain, and she said, before hanging up abruptly, "And you know what's next." But no one seemed really to know what had brought the agents up from Denver in the first place. It was shocking news, but I didn't know the men and so I didn't much care beyond the fact that perhaps a killer was loose in my backyard. The agents' names were Begay and Toliver and they were relatively young.

. . .

Hanson, the deputy from the sheriff's office, was a nice kid who had been a state wrestling champion, his mother had told me in the store one day as her son rolled by in his squad car. I could tell he was still shaken from having found Begay and Toliver face down in a scummy, shallow cove on the east side of the lake. His young face showed distress and his husky voice was unsteady as he said, "These fellers from the state police want to ask you a few questions. This here are Jacoby and Taylor."

The state police were wearing western suits and striped ties and cowboy hats. I stepped back to let them enter. They wiped their black cowboy boots and did.

"Live here alone, do you?" the larger man named Jacoby asked.

"Yes," I said.

Hanson, the deputy, sat by the stove and warmed his hands.

Taylor walked across the room, scrutinizing things, peeking around things on tables and touching things with one finger as if that allowed him to see more. He stopped at my fly-tying table, touched the vise. "Do a lot of fishing, do you?"

Jacoby sat on a stool in the kitchen and looked into the mug from which I'd just drunk tea. "I'm sure you've heard about the FBI men, haven't you?"

"Yes."

Taylor made another pass through the room. He was like a bat whispering through an attic.

"You didn't happen to see them, did you?" Jacoby asked.

"No."

"You remember the last time you went fishing, do you?" Taylor asked, rounding the stove.

"Like it was yesterday," I said. They stared at me and I stared back at them. "It was yesterday. Afternoon." I looked at young Hanson.

"You didn't see anything odd, did you?" from Jacoby.

"I fish the creeks," I said. "I seldom get over to the lake."

"He didn't ask you where you fished, did he?" Taylor.

"No."

"Go by the lake, did you?" Jacoby.

"No. I just told you that."

"See anybody around here, did you?" Jacoby.

Jacoby looked at Taylor and said, "Remember when the coroner put the time of death, do you?"

"He put it at over a week ago, didn't he?" Taylor said.

"See anybody in the woods around here last week, did you?" Jacoby asked me.

Their questions were starting to get me confused and so I started to go with the flow.

"Just the usual, I did," I said.

"Gonna tell me who's usual, are you?" Jacoby.

"I saw Hanson and I saw the Fish and Game officer, I did."

Jacoby and Taylor exchanged glances. Taylor frowned at me. "Making fun of us, are you?"

"No, I'm not, am I?"

"Cut it out, will you?" Jacoby said.

I looked again to Hanson. "Deputy, hear me doing anything, do you?"

"See the FBI men, did you?" Jacoby.

"Saw them, I didn't." Me.

"See anyone unusual or strange, did you?" Taylor.

I looked at the state police, then said, "I didn't see anyone except Hanson and the warden."

The officers seemed to breathe more easily. Jacoby got up and gave me a card. "Call us if you think of anything, will you?"

.   .   .

Came to the Hills in 1833 seven of us DeLacompt, Ezra Kind, G.W. Wood, T. Brown, R. Kent, Wm. King, Indian Crow. All died but me Ezra Kind. Killed by Indians beyond the high hill got our gold in 1834. Got all the gold we could carry our ponies got by Indians I have lost my gun and nothing to eat and Indians hunting me.

.   .   .

That night, after the visit of the state police and my probably ill-advised mocking of them, I fell asleep in my chair as I did so many nights, feeling a little lonely as I did so many nights but thinking that it wasn't so bad, thinking that it was actually pretty good. My head was throbbing and I counted the throbs until I was asleep and there in my sleep I saw the face of an old Indian man. I realized there in the dream that it was Unidentified Indian and I asked him why he was in my dream and he said, "Shut up and keep dreaming." I woke up.

.   .   .

Hiram Kills Enemy was standing on the porch of Louise Yellow Calf's house. I had parked in the driveway and was still some thirty yards from the house and no one had yet spoken to me, but I knew it was Hiram Kills Enemy. He was a small man with two gray braids falling to the middle of his back.

"Who are you?" he asked, breaking off his conversation with Big Junior and another man.

"My name is Robert Hawks. I'm an acquaintance of Louise."

"Hello, Robert," Big Junior said. "Have you thought about selling your truck?"

"You know about the Buffalo soldiers?" Kills Enemy asked. "They were colored soldiers who fought against us. The white men sent them to do their dirty work. You know about them?"

"Yes, sir," I said. "I know a little."

"Are you a Buffalo soldier?"

I shook my head, wanting to smile.

Big Junior said, "Robert ain't no Buffalo soldier."

"He looks like one," Hiram said, and then his serious face cracked with a small smile. "He looks like he's from that Tenth Cavalry. What about your grandfather?"

"How is Louise's mother?" I asked them, passing over his joking question.

"I don't know," Hiram said. "She won't let me inside the house. She's afraid of me." He said it as if it were not an odd thing, not a thing to be embarrassed about.

"Go on inside, Robert," Big Junior said. He said my name as if he liked the sound of it, not quite rolling the R.

I stepped onto the porch. "You're Hiram?" I asked.

Hiram nodded, surprised that I knew his name. He shook my hand. "This is Wilson." He indicated the third man to whom I nodded hello. Hiram looked away from me toward the mountain and said something in Plata to Wilson.

I knocked as I entered the house. The smell of food, particularly frying meat, filled the air. The walls were covered with photographs and the floor was littered with magazines that I looked at while I stepped over them; I saw most of them were Archie comic books. Then I saw one of the children curled up in a corner of the sofa. She was watching television.

I stood silently.

She raised a hand and waved to me.

"Is Louise here?"

"She's in back."

Just then Louise came into the room. She smiled on seeing me and I relaxed somewhat. "Come on back," she said, without saying hello or asking me what the hell I was doing there. "Come on." I followed the little woman down a short, dim hallway and into a brightly lit kitchen. The food smell hung in the air with the buzzing of the fluorescent light. Mary Brown was sitting at the table across from another old woman who sat in a wheelchair.

"Robert, this is my mother, Old Woman," Louise said. "Old Woman, this is Robert."

"Hello, Robert," Old Woman said.

"I'm pleased to meet you, Old Woman," I said. The words *Old Woman* did not come off my tongue easily and I longed for something else to call her. She motioned to the empty chair adjacent to hers and I sat down. Louise also sat at the table. Mary Brown reached over and touched my arm briefly, then said, "Thank you for driving me to the hospital."

I nodded, then said to Old Woman, "How are you feeling today?"

"Better than they said I would."

We sat without talking for several minutes. Louise got up and turned down the heat under a pot.

"What are you making?" I asked her.

"Chokecherry gravy."

"Have you ever had chokecherry gravy?" Mary Brown asked me. I shook my head.

"Give him some," Mary Brown said to Louise.

·   ·   ·

It was nearly dark when Louise and I stepped out into the backyard. A cord of wood was stacked neatly along the wire fence and in front of it was a stack of long wooden poles, about fifteen feet long and tapering. Louise was wearing only a sweater and was cold, I could tell, but I didn't offer my jacket.

"I suppose you heard about the FBI agents," I said. "It's real big news, I guess."

"I heard." She picked up a stick from the ground and began to peel its bark.

"They were killed last week."

Louise nodded.

"They were killed about the time you were at my place," I said, feeling clumsy.

"What are you getting at?" she asked.

"I want to know what you were doing up there near my place." I looked at her eyes.

"Nothing, I told you."

"Louise." I stopped. "The state police came to my cabin to question me."

She stopped peeling her stick.

"I didn't tell them I gave you a ride. I didn't tell them I saw you. I don't know why, but I didn't."

"You could have told them," she said. "You can tell anybody anything you want to."

"So, you think I should give—" I took the card from my pocket and looked at it—"Officer Taylor a call and tell him I happened to forget to mention that you were up there in the snow with no boots, no coat, and no way home?"

"Why don't you?" she asked.

It came to me then that I just couldn't open up to the FBI or those state cops. All I really knew was that there was a lot going on that I didn't know about. And how would I now explain my initial story, or rather my initial lie?

"So, what's going on?" I asked.

"I didn't shoot them," she said.

"I didn't think you did."

"I didn't see them either," she said. She dropped the stick.

"I believe you," I said.

"Did you shoot them, Robert?"

I glanced at her face and let out a brief chuckle. I kicked at a rock with my toe. "What were you doing out there, Louise?"

"Let it go, Robert."

I felt myself becoming angry, but I put it aside. I didn't understand what was going on. I didn't much like Louise and it was clear she didn't give a fuck about me.

·   ·   ·

Article 4. [The government of the United States and the said Indians, being mutually desirous that the latter shall be located in a country where they may eventually become self-supporting and acquire the arts of civilized life, it is therefore agreed that the said Indians shall select a delegation of the principal men from its band, who shall, without delay, visit the Indian Territory under the guidance and protection of suitable persons, to be appointed by that purpose by the Department of Interior, with a view to selecting therein a permanent home for the said Indians. If such delegation shall make a selection which shall be satisfactory to themselves, the people whom they represent, and to the United States, then the said Indians agree that they will remove to the country so selected within one year from this date. And the said Indians do further agree in all things to submit themselves to such beneficent plans as the government may provide for them in the selection of a country suitable for a permanent home, where they may live like white men.]

·   ·   ·

I drove directly back to my cabin after seeing Louise without even entertaining the thought of stopping at the junction for food. When morning found me I was dressed in the previous day's clothes, feeling that I smelled slightly, and sitting in the chair in front of the stove. I was starving and had nothing to prepare. I drove down the road to the diner. It was about seven-thirty and freezing cold.

Holly, the waitress, said, "Sit anywhere," even though I'd been in there over twenty times and knew to sit anywhere. Holly brought me coffee and a menu.

"Thanks, Holly," I said as I sat in a booth.

"Name's not Holly," she said.

I looked at her. "Your name's not Holly? Wasn't it Holly last week?"

"It was. But not now." She tapped her pad with her pencil. "You see, I'm getting married."

"I see," I said. "But wouldn't that change your last name and wouldn't that happen after you got married?"

She nodded. "I'm marrying Sam Wood." She waited for me to figure it out.

"Ah," I said. "So, what's your new name?"

"Laurel."

"Much better," I said.

"Do you really like it?"

I nodded.

"What'll it be?" she asked.

"I'll have the number two. Wheat toast."

The bell on the door rang and I looked up to see young Hanson, the deputy, come into the restaurant. He removed his hat as he entered, spotted me, and came over to my booth. He sat in front of me.

"Deputy," I said. Everyone called Hanson "deputy." In fact, I didn't know his first name.

"Hey, Robert. Okay if I sit with you?"

"Of course it is."

Hanson waved to get the waitress's attention, then turned back to me. "You gonna stay the winter?"

"Looks like it."

"You're a hydrologist, aren't you?"

The waitress came and poured Hanson a cup of coffee.

"Thanks, Laurel," Hanson said. "I'll have the special."

Laurel smiled and walked back to the window between the counter and the kitchen.

"Yes, I'm a hydrologist," I said.

"Do you like it? I mean, does it pay well?"

I nodded to the first question. "It pays all right," I told him. "I'm on leave right now. That's the nice thing. I get leaves every few years. So I can hang out up here for a while."

"Sounds good," Hanson said, but his words sounded thin.

"Have you heard any more about the FBI guys?" I asked.

Hanson shook his head. "They were shot, both of them, in the chest. Close up, you know? I never seen anything like that."

"It must have been awful," I said.

Hanson nodded slightly, as if he hadn't quite heard me. He found his coffee and drank some. "I've been a deputy for three years. In all that time, the closest I ever came to a dead person was that truck driver who got paralyzed last summer. Were you here when that rig went off at Dog Pass?"

"I heard about it," I said. "Any idea who killed them?"

Hanson shrugged. "I wouldn't know. I don't even know who's in charge of the investigation. The state cops hate the FBI and the FBI talk to us like we're not fit to peek in the bowl at their turds."

I nodded.

Hanson studied me for a long second. "Somebody's going to come talk to you again, to ask you more questions."

"Why is that?"

Laurel brought our breakfast, then left.

"Why are they coming to talk to me?" I asked.

"One, because you live up there near where it happened . . ."

"And two?" I took a bite of toast.

"Two, because those state cops didn't like you one little bit. You know, Robert, you've got kind of an attitude."

"That's been suggested to me before," I said.

"Well, it don't bother me none," Hanson said, "but, jeez, you gotta watch it with some people."

. . .

I opened the letter as I was driving away from Clara's store. It was from Karen; I thought of disposing it unopened and unread, but I didn't.

> *Dear Robert,*
>
> *I hope this letter finds you relaxed by your fishing and enjoying the coming of winter. I'm doing well here alone in the city. Work is fine, except that Sheila, the witch, keeps accusing me of getting projects done on time just to make her look bad. I laugh it off though, knowing that of course she's right.*
>
> *I miss you, you big idiot. Why won't you call me? I'm sorry if I caused you to be anxious and I'm sorry I'm so crazy. Actually, I'm not sorry. Why should I be sorry about something I can't help? Why aren't you sorry? You have got some nerve leaving me here is this sucky city and making me feel like it's my fault. Why are you being so cruel to me? I'm so mad at you. Please know how much I love you, how much I care, even though you couldn't care less about me or my feelings. Fishing is all you think about. If I had*

gills instead of breasts, maybe you'd be more interested.
You know what you can do with that bamboo rod you're so
crazy about. Go to hell, Robert Hawks! I love you so much.
Please, come back. Please, call. I won't be insane anymore.

~~*Love*~~

Love, Karen

·   ·   ·

Primary descriptions of watershed shape and geologic configurations
were obtained from field investigations. Here again, observations agreed
with Rocker's work. The dominant characteristics in the Plata Moun-
tain watershed are the west face of Plata Mountain; Silly Man Ridge;
and the entry of Skinner, Dog, and Hell-hole Canyons into the water-
shed from the west and north.

Plata Creek was found to be dry above the entrance of Dog Canyon,
to achieve roughly 9 cubic feet per second of flow from Dog, and then to
lose and gain flow for about three miles below the confluence of Silly
Man and Red Creeks. The channel of Plata Creek occupies a shallow
trough and wide flood plain between dramatically undercut slopes of
older terraces.

·   ·   ·

In my dream I was on the aircraft carrier *Theodore Roosevelt* and I
was wearing a blue cap that read *CVN 71* over the brim that
shaded my eyes. I couldn't see the cap, but I knew what was written on it. I was in the mess and I couldn't see any water, nor could
I see planes, but I knew where I was. I was sitting across the gray
table from a big red-faced man who was eating little green grapes
and he was smiling between bites, pointing at me with a sausage
finger and saying, "You're in on this somehow and when I find
out how, I'm gonna have your liver for breakfast." I told him to
go fuck himself, then walked out of the galley, and started climb-

ing ladders. I climbed ladder after ladder, higher and higher into the ship, thinking at the top of each one that I would find the deck, but I didn't. All I found was another ladder and another ladder. Finally I met a man on a ladder, an Indian in traditional dress, beaded moccasins and a buffalo robe over his shoulders, but he had no paint on his face. I told him I was looking for the deck. He told me he'd been there and that there was no water. "It's truly something to see," he said, "this big ship sitting in the middle of a mud plane. See, you can't feel the water." I attended to my legs and indeed there was no motion, no movement of the ocean, only stillness, an unrelenting stillness that would not stop, a stillness I hated, a stillness I wanted gone, a stillness that woke me up.

I sat up in bed and looked out my window. I'd left on the outside light and I could see that it was snowing.

.   .   .

The strength of my grandfather's personality had a delimiting effect on all those around him except my father and me. Most people were badly put off by his vocal and immediate repudiation of all things Christian, but oddly, in spite of the proclivity of the black community toward Christianity, he didn't alienate his patients. It was perhaps the case that his antireligious tendencies seemed so abstract that they were not taken seriously, but rather as an idiosyncratic function of the brilliant doctor. My father kept his sentiments more to himself, nodding when the family of patients asked him if prayer would help and saying, "How could it hurt?"

.   .   .

Big Junior stepped with heavy feet into my cabin as if he was way too big to fit. The fact of the matter was that Big Junior was not all that big. He was a little shorter than me at about 5 feet 10 inches and weighed maybe 190 pounds, so he was stout, certainly, but hardly big. Nonetheless, I greeted him by saying, "Come on in, Big Junior." I looked at the sky as he came in and saw that it was clear and bright. Big Junior had driven up the mountain in a baby blue 1963 Cadillac convertible, the color of the sky.

Big Junior said, "Louise said you had a nice place. This is a nice place. It's in a nice spot and it's a nice house. Nice house, nice truck. You're doing all right."

"Thanks," I said. "That's some car you drove up in."

"That thing belongs to Wilson. Ugly, ain't it? But it runs. Runs all the time. Can't turn it off almost. Wilson won it in a rodeo way back when."

"I see," I said as I closed the door. "It's ugly, all right."

"Don't tell him that. Wilson loves that thing." Big Junior walked around the room, in a manner not unlike the state policemen who had visited days earlier. He paused at my tying table, dragging his finger through the pheasant tail feathers I kept standing in a jar. "You make your own flies?"

"Yep."

He picked up an elk's hair caddis and looked at it closely. "That's really something. It looks just like a bug. If I was a trout, I'd bite this for sure."

"Do you fish?" I asked him.

"Never been."

I let out a sudden chuckle. "You live here in this place and you've never been fishing?"

"That's right." He sat in the soft chair in front of the stove as if to try it out. "This is nice."

I picked up a log from the pile and opened the stove door; the heat brushed my face and felt good. Big Junior leaned forward and watched me closely. I watched him watching me while I put in the wood.

"What are you doing here, Big Junior?" I asked, closing the door and turning down the latch.

"Hiram asked me to come see you," he said.

"Hiram Kills Enemy?"

Big Junior said, "Yes," and continued to move his eyes around the room.

"So, why did he send you?"

"He wanted me to ask you something."

I waited while Big Junior leaned back and seemed to enjoy the softness of the chair. His stout body was squirming its way into especially comfortable spots.

"Yes?" I asked.

"Would you take me fishing?"

"Anytime," I told him and he said what about right then and I became just a bit short with him. "Big Junior, what does Hiram want you to ask me?"

"Oh yeah, he wants you to see him at his house tomorrow. He lives by the river. He's got a nice place, too."

"Did he tell you why?"

Big Junior shook his head. He frowned and in his face I could see the subject change. "Let's go fishing."

. . .

So we went fishing. Big Junior's feet were smaller than mine and he didn't mind using an old pair of hip-waders. I put a graphite six-weight in his hands and tried to teach him how to roll cast. The air was icy and just a short distance up the mountain the air was not so clear. A freezing rain was falling gently on us and causing the guides on our rods to clog with ice. I told Big Junior I didn't expect to catch any fish. I told him that I never expected to catch any fish and he laughed at that. I had to tie the flies onto the leader for him, because it turned out that Big Junior had enormous fingers, not so much long but fat like bratwurst, and it was clear that he would not be able to manipulate the tiny flies. Big Junior was a bit wild with the rod and I tried to stand clear of him when he attempted casts. It was unfortunate that he too could not stand clear, because he managed to hook his ear with a very strange motion that was preceded by him saying, "Looky here."

"Hold still," I said, trying to get his hand away from his ear so I could inspect the wound.

He swore a few times and I told him to let me see it. He moved his hand. The hook had gone cleanly through his lobe and luckily, although it must have hurt like hell, it hadn't ripped him at all when he tugged at the line.

"Get it out," he said.

"I'm going to have to cut it off," I said, reaching into my pocket for my wire cutters.

"No!"

"Not your ear, Big Junior. The hook."

"Just pull it out," he said.

"It's got a barb on it," I said. "I can't pull it out without ripping your ear. So I'm going to snip off the barb." I showed him the wire cutters. "Then it will slide right out." He didn't make a noise as I cut through the hook, although I could tell it really hurt.

"There," I said.

He rubbed his ear. "This is a dangerous sport."

I agreed.

. . .

"Don't shoot," I said softly. The barrel of the revolver didn't quite touch my seventeen-year-old head, but I felt its coldness none-theless. The second and third cops circled, making comments about the length of our Afro hairdos and the fact that we were wearing army fatigue jackets.

"What did we do?" my friend Marvin asked, his face pressed against the hood of the car, his eyes on mine.

"What are you boys doing over here?" one of the cops asked.

"We were at a party," I said.

The cop, I remember he smelled of Brut, kicked my feet farther apart and asked, "What kind of party?"

"Just a party," Marvin said.

"This your car?" another cop.

"Yes," I said.

"Mind if we search it?"

And then I could feel my grandfather and my father inside my head. I raised up, I think to the astonishment of the police, and turned around. I looked past the pistol at the first cop's chest. "No, I don't mind, Officer Toby, badge number three-six-nine. Search my car and explain probable cause to me while you do it."

The third cop who had arrived in a car by himself came and stood close to me, his breath on my face. "You're a smart one, are you?" he said.

"Robert," I heard Marvin complain behind me.

I looked at the cop with the breath and I said, "Fuck you." That's the last thing I remembered of that evening. The next morning, as my father escorted me out of the police station, I saw the wall just inside the door streaked with red and I knew it was my blood and when the air hit me outside I had never felt so free in my life.

·   ·   ·

We walked down the creek, stepping carefully along the rocky bank all the way to the lake. Ice was forming in the slow water between the rocks near the edge. We reached the lake and stopped, looked across it. The snow settled and disappeared on its surface.

"This is where they found those FBIs," Big Junior said, looking at the ground by his feet and then into the shallow water at the bank.

"Right here?" I asked.

"Around here someplace," he said. "I'm an FBI. Did you know that?" He studied my confusion. "I'm a full-blooded Indian." He laughed. "I heard those FBIs were bad. I heard they wasn't no good."

"How so?" I asked. My hands were getting really cold and I found myself pinching under my nails for feeling.

"They were crooked, people are saying." His words were short, barked almost quietly. "I'd shoot any FBI if I had the chance." He held up his hand like a gun and said, "Bang." Big Junior nodded. "They're the government, right? Well, I'm at war with the government. You know what I mean?"

I didn't say anything.

"You are too."

I looked at the shallows of the lake. "They found them floating face down in the water," I said. "They were shot at close range."

Big Junior nodded like the information was useful.

"What's Louise into?" I asked.

"We didn't catch any fish," he said.

"It's probably too cold," I told him.

"We'll try again when it's warmer."

.　.　.

Article 11. The aforesaid tribe acknowledges its dependence on the Government of the United States, and promises to be friendly with all the citizens thereof, and to commit no depredations or other violence upon such citizens. And should any one or more violate this pledge, and the fact be proved to the satisfaction of the President, the property shall be returned, or, in default thereof, or if injured or destroyed, compensation may be made by the Government out of the annuities. The aforesaid tribe is hereby bound to deliver such offenders to the proper authorities for trial and punishment, and are held responsible, in its tribal capacity, to make reparation for depredations so committed.

The tongue has mucous and serous glands. The mucous glands are located in the back, to the rear of the circumvallate papillae, although they are also found at the marginal parts. The serous glands are found only at the back of the tongue, near the taste buds. The fibrous septum consists of a vertical layer of fibrous tissue, extending throughout the entire length of the middle line of the tongue, from the base to the apex, although not quite reaching the dorsum. It is thicker behind than in front, and occasionally contains a small fibro-cartilage about a quarter of an inch in length. It is well displayed by making a vertical section across the organ.

3

The woman from the FBI was sitting in my cabin and asking me point blank if I had given a ride to a small Indian woman on Tuesday of the week the agents were killed. I looked at the woman; her hard eyes were searching me for an answer or some movement of a facial muscle that might tell her something, and I wondered briefly where she kept her gun and then I wondered why I hadn't concerned myself with that question when the state cops were in my house. But I knew where they kept their guns.

"Did you give anyone a ride that day?" Special Agent Gladys Davies asked me again.

"No," I said.

"I have a witness who says you did."

"I drove by a woman," I said, "but I didn't pick her up."

"Was she a small woman?"

"I don't know what you mean."

"Little. Under five feet tall. Under four and a half feet tall."

I shook my head.

"You're sure?"

I nodded.

"Do you know a woman who fits that description?" she asked.

In my mind I was thinking "what description?" but I said, "I know some short people."

"This woman would be an Indian."

"I see."

"Do you know any really short Indians?"

"Do you mean like midget short?" I asked.

"Yes."

"No."

"Have you ever seen such an individual?"

"You mean, a midget?"

"A midget Indian woman."

"I don't know. How would I know if she were Indian?"

Special Agent Davies stood up and shook my hand. "Well, thank you for your time. I'll probably be coming back to talk to you again. You have a good day now."

I waved to her like a moron as she drove away.

My tongue felt huge and dry in my mouth, as if it might choke me. Perhaps it already had. I found it difficult to swallow.

. . .

The lie was a great big fat one and I had more than a little sinking feeling. What was worse was that I did not know why I had lied. I had no real reason to suspect that Louise Yellow Calf was involved in the deaths of the two FBI agents, but things were not clear with her. In fact, I did have some idea why I had lied, although knowledge of a feeling doesn't make it rational. I recognized that I was almost pathologically incapable of imparting anything but basic information to the FBI. Had she been asking me if I had seen the purse snatcher run past me on the street I might have answered her truthfully, but the whole feel of this thing was muddled and dicey. Although it would be dusk in just a couple of hours, and the sky promised more snow and the temperature seemed to be dropping like a shot bird, I decided to make the long drive down to Plata and to Louise's house.

The sun was kissing the top of the horizon and the house was dark when I got there. No cars were parked in the yard. The wind whipped some loose paper across the drive and over the pasture to the east. A white-faced barn owl was sitting on a nearby telephone line and he was watching me, his face moving with me as I approached the porch. I climbed the steps to the door and knocked; the wood felt extra hard against my cold knuckles. I knocked again. Hearing no movement inside, I walked around the house looking for any kind of light or sign of presence. It struck me that perhaps the old woman had again been taken ill and that they were all at the hospital. I walked into the backyard and saw the stacked wood and the pile of poles sitting under a partially melted overlay of snow. I knocked on the back door. Snow started to fall and I zipped my parka up to my neck. I went back to the front porch and sat on the steps to wait for a while. The owl was still there, still watching.

. . .

When freezing, one thinks. I thought about my gut reaction to police. Young Hanson didn't bother me; he was simply young Hanson, ex-wrestler, son of a woman who liked to chat in the market. But the state cops, with their attitudes and their swaggers and their stares, were a different matter. They were the same cops. They were the cops who said I looked like the 6-foot, 8-inch, 250-pound robbery suspect when I was driving home from college.

They were the cops who pushed my face into the hood of my car while they checked my license and registration; one was pushing while the other stood back with his drawn pistol pointed at my head, again, just as my father told me it would happen. I kept my mouth shut that time. I didn't want to have that stupid, bloody, free feeling once more; I didn't want to hear the cop asking why I didn't say "sir," calling me "boy."

And the woman from the FBI. Well, she was from the FBI. That seemed enough.

. . .

Half an hour passed and it was just too cold to continue waiting. My back was tightening and my face burned and hurt from the icy wind. It occurred to me again that they were probably at the hospital with another emergency; the old woman was probably stretched out on a gurney with some misdiagnosed, deadly disease that Hiram Kills Enemy had already told her she didn't have. I could see them sitting in the lounge, Mary Brown, Big Junior and his fat wife, and Louise, and although I was feeling more than a little desperate, I was not going there. Instead I drove from Plata to the village of Rivertown and went into a tavern called the Stirrup. I stopped there because I liked the pun and I'd heard the food was decent. Moderately loud, two-stepping country music leaked out when a couple left. I noticed that the snow was falling heavily as I walked across the parking lot. Big flakes landed on my face and troubled my vision.

Inside the smoky place I sat in a booth with green vinyl seats and a pink tabletop and waited until the waitress, who was wearing some jeans she'd put on as a young child and had grown into, came over. She asked, "What d'ya want?"

"Chili and fries. And a Coke."

She nodded and wiggled away through the crowd.

There were a couple of Indian men at the bar who were laughing and joking with a tall blond woman who had applied her makeup with a palette knife. And there was me. Everyone else was white and I understood why the reservation had felt comfortable to me, in spite of my appearing as a Buffalo soldier, and it was a weird, kind of embarrassing, revelation.

Two bodies slid into the booth opposite me. Jacoby and Taylor, the state policemen, filled the green seat.

"Looky what the cat drug in, why don't you?" Jacoby said.

"Just dropping in for a little bite to eat, are you?" Taylor said.

"You wouldn't have some other reason to be down here near the reservation, would you?" Jacoby.

"Visiting somebody, are you?" Taylor.

"A woman, is it?" Jacoby.

"Hello, Mr. Hawks." This was a new voice, a woman's voice, Special Agent Davies's voice. She looked at the two men. "Sorry to interrupt, but Mr. Hawks and I have an appointment."

Jacoby and Taylor didn't speak, just raised their stiff, tightly wound bodies out of their seats and stepped mechanically away. They looked back and muttered something unintelligible, but Davies didn't seem to care.

"Strange meeting you here," I said to Davies as she sat down across from me.

"It's a small place," she said. She was wearing makeup and wearing it fairly badly. Her eyes were imprisoned in black and her cheeks wore red streaks. "What brings you to town?"

"I heard the chili was good here," I said.

"Must be great to get you down here in this weather."

"Things are slow in these parts," I said.

"I'm from Indiana originally," Davies said.

"So you understand slow."

"Oh, yes."

I nodded. "I hear tell that's a pretty flat place."

"Flat enough."

The waitress came and looked at Davies. "You want any food, honey?"

"The chili," Davies said. "I hear it's good."

"The chili sucks," the waitress said.

"Why didn't you say that when I ordered it?" I asked.

"I don't like your looks."

I chuckled at first and then, looking at her face, I came to understand. I said, "You mean the fact that I'm black."

"Possibly."

She surely didn't matter enough to make me mad, but I said, as I got up to leave, "Well, Miss almost-GED-nineteen-seventy-eight, I'll be going now."

"Fine with me."

Davies got up with me.

"You don't have to go, honey," the waitress said.

"Yes, I do," said Davies with a kind of laugh. "The view and the stench in here are awful."

I wasn't too upset by the waitress and I wasn't too terribly surprised at Davies's reaction, although as she stood to leave with me I noticed that she was just a little bit drunk. In fact, I found her allying herself with me a bit disconcerting and I distrusted her.

"Is there another bar we can go to?" she asked, once we were out in the parking lot.

"There's one a couple of blocks into town," I said. "The food is only mediocre, however, not average like this place."

"Sounds good enough to me."

I didn't want her company, but I had it now. "I'll drive," I said, thinking that even though it was a short drive, she'd been drinking and also I didn't want her to be in control. "We can come back and pick up your car later."

We got into my truck and went to the next place, a smaller place, more of a joint than the first. It had a small neon sign out front, some fat cowboys playing pool in the back, and Patsy Cline singing on a weak-speakered jukebox.

"Now, this is more like it," Davies said.

"Where do you want to sit, Inspector?" I asked.

"Call me Gladys."

"Where do you want to sit, Inspector Gladys?"

"How about that booth?" She pointed to a booth tucked away in the corner. "And it's Special Agent."

I followed her to it and sat down across from her. I pulled the menus from between the napkin dispenser and the wall and handed her one.

"So, what's mediocre?" she asked.

"Everything."

The waitress came with glasses of water. "Anything to drink?" she asked.

"Beer," Davies said. "And bring me a fried-egg sandwich on white bread and a little mustard."

I closed my menu. "Coffee for me. I'd like a burger, rare, with cheese and no onions." I watched the white nurse shoes of the waitress as she walked away, then looked to Davies. "An egg sandwich?" I said.

"I like eggs," she said, leaning back. "So, tell me about the reservation."

"I don't know anything to tell."

"You're a hydrologist. You ever work with the Plata? You know, on all this water stuff? Tell me about that."

I shook my head. "I described the geological features of the Plata Mountain drainage, but for an environmental organization. I don't get involved in political stuff. I'm just a scientist."

"So, you know these mountains pretty well, don't you? I mean, you live here."

I nodded. "There are a lot of people who know them better than I do. I know which way the water drains and runs. That's about all I know. You want me to tell you about the nature of the sediments or terrace formation?"

The waitress brought my coffee and Davies's beer.

"You're probably wondering how I came to be in the FBI," she said and pulled from her bottle, ignoring the frosted glass mug that came with it.

"Not really," I said.

"I went to fucking law school, met a cute guy, got knocked up, lost the cute guy, dropped out of fucking law school, lost the baby, got mad, joined the FBI." She looked away; a crack seemed to be showing in her chitinous exoskeleton.

"The classic American story." I waited while she took another pull on her beer. "Are you drunk?" I asked.

"I was drunk two weeks ago and it felt a lot like this."

"What happened then?"

"I passed out."

"Is that likely to happen tonight?" I asked.

"Not after this one, but after the third, yes."

The egg sandwich came and was pushed aside. I ate my burger and Davies turned out to be true to her word. She drained her third bottle, put her head on the table, and never came up. What I thought as I studied the top of her head on the table was how much I truly disliked her, in spite of her clumsy attempt at decency.

. . .

The flood plain of the Plata Mountain watershed is usually sandy and exhibits a moderate amount of hull material that appears to consist of calcium carbonate and clay from contributing soils. This kind of hull matter typically tends to decrease the roughness of the channel. The sandy alluvium exhibits ripple marks, indicative of high velocities and erosional action by the stream. Occasional boulders are found in the middle of the stream along with flood debris, including trees, logs, and brush that form with soil and rock into irregularly shaped swellings in the flood plain.

. . .

So there I was in lily white Rivertown with an unconscious Caucasian woman who had a badge and, no doubt, a gun in her purse. The waitress came to the table, stopped and looked at Davies.

"She done passed out, honey," the woman said. "You're going

to have to get her out of here. We don't allow no drunks in here once they've passed out."

I didn't say anything. There was not much to say. I tried to lift Davies from behind to drag her out, but that became sloppy right away and seemed not to be working. I took her arm and pulled her over my shoulder and carried her out fireman style with all sorts of hoots and hollers following me through the door. Outside, I loaded the drunk woman into my truck through the driver's-side door and pushed her all the way over so that her head rested against the opposite window. As I turned the key I thought that all I would need right then would be to have my truck fail to start. But it did start and I realized as I pulled out of the parking space that I didn't know where to take this catatonic FBI agent. It wasn't going to do much good to drive her back to her car and I didn't know where she was staying. And, finally, I would not be calling the FBI in Denver and have them misunderstand my story about having in my possession an unconscious agent of theirs. I turned north toward Plata Mountain and my house.

I turned the heat on high hoping that she would wake up, but the way she moaned suggested that I had only made her feel warm and cozy. She twisted her body and then fell over, her head landing in my lap. She talked in her sleep, but I could not make out any words, although I could feel her breath on my thigh through the fabric of my trousers. All of a sudden she shouted, "Freeze!" and I nearly lost control of the truck. I turned up the heat again.

.   .   .

At my house the snow was considerably deep and I had to shovel through a small drift to reach the door. I worked up a good sweat that made me feel just a little more alive. I then pulled Davies from the cab and carried her, over my shoulder, inside where I put her down in front of the cold stove. She felt heavier this time; perhaps she was more deeply unconscious. I covered her with a blanket and got a fire going. Her breathing was even and I felt confident that she was okay, so I left her in the big chair with her feet up and I went to bed.

. . .

You may rest assured that I shall adhere to the just and humane policy towards the Indians which I have commenced. In this spirit I have recommended them to quit their possessions on this side of the Mississippi, and go to a country to the west where there is every probability that they will always be free from the mercenary influence of white men, and undisturbed by the local authority of the states: Under such circumstances the General Government can exercise a parental control over their interests and possibly perpetuate their race.

. . .

I didn't sleep well that night. I had trouble at first, tossing and turning and waking to the sound of my guest's stirrings. I had the fleeting thought that she might come and attempt to share my covers, or in a dream walk in and shoot me, or, worse, kiss me. As far as I know, the former never happened. When I did find sleep it was deep and unmoving. I was awakened by icy air and when I sat up and focused I damn near screamed. There was Karen, wearing a godawful full-length fiber-filled parka, standing in the open doorway, hurling clothes out into the snow. I watched this, her flinging out a bra, then going back and grabbing a sock and tossing that out. I heard the shower and slowly began to piece it all together. Davies was in the shower. Her clothes were on the floor. The madwoman was in the doorway and I was standing next to the kitchen counter in my boxers, rubbing my head.

"Karen," I said. "What are you doing?"

"I've been such a fool," she said. "I trusted you. I thought you were up here fishing and trying to find yourself. I should have seen it. I should have known."

"Karen, slow down."

"Slow down? I'll take it about as slow as you and Ms. Clean in there."

I pulled on my robe and put some more wood in the stove. "This isn't what you think."

"No, then what is it?"

"The woman in the bathroom is an FBI agent who's in the middle of an investigation."

"Yeah, right. And what's she investigating? Your missing cock?" Karen slammed the door and stood in the center of the room. She spotted Davies's handbag and moved toward it.

"I wouldn't touch that if I were you," I said. "She *is* an FBI special agent, so if I were you . . ."

"Well, you're not me. I'm me. I'm the only one who's me around here. Not you, not her, just me. Do you fucking understand?"

I nodded. "Still, I wouldn't open that bag."

"Fuck you. I want to know the tramp's name." She opened the bag, pushed in her hand, and came out with a .38 revolver. "Oh, my god," she said. "She carries a gun. What kind of low-life slut are you ditching me for?"

"Put it back."

The sound from the shower ceased. Karen looked at the bathroom door. "She carries a gun, Robert."

"She's an FBI agent," I repeated.

The bathroom door opened and Davies came out; her body was wrapped in a towel, her hair was wet and uncovered. She stopped, her hair dripping on the floor and making puddles by her feet. Karen's hand tightened reflexively about the pistol and the barrel came up pointed at Davies.

"I would put that down if I were you," Davies said.

Karen's face was frozen; her eyes were like saucers.

"Gladys, I'd like you to meet my friend, Karen."

Karen pointed the gun at me. "Your friend?"

"You're not my friend?"

"Give me the gun, Karen," Davies said and she took a small step toward her.

"Stay away from me!" Karen shouted.

Davies stopped.

I sat down on the stool by the stove.

"How can you just sit there!" Karen shouted at me.

"I'm sitting because if you are crazy enough to shoot me I don't want to fall far. You need help, Karen, and I can't give it to you. So, go ahead and shoot me so you can go to prison and get daily help from a prison doctor named Hilda who likes you in a way you won't like."

"I hate you!" Karen dropped the pistol on the floor and ran screaming out of the house.

Davies and I remained motionless as we listened to Karen's car engine rev up and her car roll away over the crusty snow.

"Don't ask," I said.

Davies bent and picked up her weapon and examined it, then put it carefully back into her bag. She sat in the chair in front of the stove and blew out a long sigh.

"Sorry about that," I said.

"Did I pass out?"

"Oh yeah."

"Did we?"

"Oh no."

She nodded.

"But Karen thought we did. That's why all of your clothes are outside in the snow."

She looked around the chair, saw only one of her shoes, and picked it up. "Shit."

"Yep." I stood up and refastened the belt of my robe. "I'll get my boots and collect your things."

Davies was holding her shaking head in her hands. "I don't believe this."

"Neither do I," I said.

I pulled on some jeans, a dirty T-shirt, and boots and waded through the snow to get Davies's clothes. They were soaked of course and I felt more than a little strange holding her bra and panties. I took them to her.

"Here they are," I said.

She pulled her face from her hands and looked at the wet clothes. "Oh, my god." She looked down again, shaking her head as if to empty it. "What time is it?"

I looked over at the clock on the counter that I had forgotten to wind and estimated. "It's about nine."

"Do you have a phone?"

"Nope."

She sighed. "Where is the nearest phone?"

"Down the mountain at the junction. I use the one at the general store."

"I've got to call my office."

"I'll drive you down there. In fact, I have to drive you to Rivertown. That's where we left your car. I would have taken you to your motel, but I didn't know which one."

"I guess I should thank you for not leaving me to freeze."

"You're welcome." I walked into the bathroom and draped her clothes over the shower rod, then came back. "I guess you'll have to wear some of my clothes."

"You don't have a dryer?" she said.

I smiled and shook my head.

"Who was that woman?"

"She was at one time a girlfriend. That's the first time I've seen her in over a month. I don't return her calls or her letters. You know the drill. I'm a dog."

"At least you know it."

. . .

Davies was a moderately large woman, but still my clothes swallowed her up, leaving her looking like she was wearing my clothes.

"You look fine," I said.

"Let's go."

"You at least have your own coat to wear," I said.

We walked out and got into my truck, worked our way through the dirt road, then skated down the badly plowed highway.

"The road people do more harm than good," I said.

"Did you shoot the agents?" Davies asked.

"No."

"Do you know who did?"

"No."

"Do you have any idea who did?"

"No."

"Are you telling me everything you know?"

"No."

She rolled down her window about half an inch and I could feel the frigid air on my side of the cab. "You ought to tell me everything you know. You could get into a lot of trouble. Do you know a woman named Louise Yellow Calf?"

"What were the FBI men doing up here?" I asked.

"That's not your business. Now, answer my question."

"No, I don't know anyone by that name." And I felt another shovel of dirt land on top of me. My heart was beating rapidly. "You don't think I'm involved, do you?" A stupid question.

"I don't know you," she said. "I hope, for your sake, that you're telling me everything you know." She looked back out the window. "Never mind about the phone. Can you just take me back to my car?"

"Sure."

.   .   .

Dog Canyon was inspected on 23 and 24 September, the field work consisting of observations and measurements from where the canyon opens into Plata Canyon to approximately 1.5 miles above the confluence of Silly Man and Red Creeks. Cross-sections were taken at high and middle elevations and at the canyon mouth, and high-water marks were noted and flood stage width was measured. (See photograph no. 6.)

The headwaters of Dog Canyon arise in the Plata Mountain sandstone, a carboniferous sandstone. The stream bed, however, is etched through limestone. The canyon's north wall is steep and so is notably different from the Hell-hole and Skinner Creeks in overall shape. Areas of the stream bed and the north wall suggest that a Halgaito tongue might be present—a red, slimy sandstone alternating with limestone and shale. Here the wall seems particularly susceptible to the loss of angular fragments caused by wind and water.

.   .   .

Davies's car was just where she had left it. Her parting words were "Again, I hope you're not holding back."

I nodded and watched her walk toward her car. She stopped and called back to me.

"I'll bring the clothes back later," she said.

I didn't want her coming back to my place, but I gave her the okay sign anyway. I didn't go home after I had watched her drive off to wherever her motel was.

4

I went back to the reservation, to Plata Township, to the house of Louise's mother. The house, in the morning light, seemed as abandoned as it had the previous night. I sat in my truck in the driveway and didn't bother to get out, just waited for someone to come out or someone else to come up to the house. I stared at the paint, at the way it curled in strips off the beams supporting the porch. No one came up the drive and no one stepped out of the house, and so I drove over to the little store at the intersection with the flashing amber traffic signal.

"Do you know Louise Yellow Calf?" I asked the young woman who was standing behind the cash register. Her hair was in one long braid that hung down over her left shoulder and was secured at the bottom by a clip with yellow and red beads.

She looked at me with her dark eyes and said, "No."

"She's very small," I said, holding my hand down to illustrate her height.

She studied my hand and then my face again. "Oh, you're talking about Very Little Woman."

"Yes," I said.

"I haven't seen her lately. Not for a week or so. Why are you looking for her?"

"She's a friend of mine," I said. "I haven't seen her for a while either and I guess I'm just a little worried."

"Well, I haven't seen her." She looked toward the back of the store.

"Do you know Hiram Kills Enemy?"

"Yes."

A couple of teenagers fell in line behind me. One held a loaf of bread. The other had a Big Hunk candy bar and a liter bottle of generic cola.

"Do you know where his house is?"

She seemed a bit tired of me. "He lives down near where the road crosses the river. Hi, Chuckie," she said to the teenager immediately behind me.

I walked to the parking lot where I leaned against my truck. It was midmorning now and I was starting to feel pretty hungry. I was feeling lost, too. I wanted to eat just so I could do something familiar. Here I was, a dormant hydrologist, trying to spend the autumn alone, trying to break up with my girlfriend, stuck in the middle of an FBI investigation of the murder of two of their agents, practically in my backyard. I'd lied to the investigating officer, without good reason, about the night of the crime and so had made myself look like a probable suspect. There I was digging myself in deeper by going to the reservation and attempting to find Louise Yellow Calf. And I wanted to locate Hiram Kills Enemy because I thought he might know something about Louise and because Big Junior had told me that the old man wanted to see me.

I drove down to the bridge over the Plata River. It was a pretty river, full of rocks and twists. Down here the flow usually slowed some and there were fewer rocks impeding its progress. There were rumors among the whites of trout of great size lurking in the river, but since it was on the reservation, they could not fish the water. That seemed right and fair to me, but the townspeople saw it, as they chose to see everything that the Indians just barely managed to hold onto, as a huge inconvenience to them. "They don't even fish the water," I'd heard men say. One of the men I'd heard say it was that pain-in-the-ass fellow from Clara's store who always wanted to know where the black hydrologist stood on the water question.

From where I was standing on the bridge I could see a couple of small shacks nestled into a stand of tall cottonwoods just back from the bank. There was a dirt road off the highway that at least pointed in that direction. I got back into my truck and followed it.

. . .

Article 9. About seven and two-fifths acres bounded as follows: Beginning at the northeast corner of lot eighty-nine, in the center of Dog Road; thence west, along the north line of said lot, fifty-four and a quarter rods; thence south, thirty-eight and a quarter rods; thence east twenty-eight and a quarter rods; thence north thirty-four rods; thence east twenty-six rods; thence north four rods, to the place of the beginning, comprising the ground heretofore used by the Plata to bury their dead, shall be patented to the supervisors of the town of Plata, to be held by them and their successors in trust for the inhabitants of said town, to be used by them as a cemetery, and the proceeds from cemetery lots and burial places to be applied in fencing, clearing, and embellishing the grounds.

. . .

The dirt lane twisted and opened up in places as if to swallow my truck. It threw me against the ceiling and into the door, and at one point I was straddling a wide ditch filled with sharp-edged rocks. By the time I had made the circuitous trip to the shacks in the stand of cottonwoods, I was sweating and a little cranky.

Hiram came out of the larger house and watched me roll to a stop. He looked at me and then back at the trail. He shook his head.

"What is it?" I asked.

"I'm impressed," he said. "Not too many people actually drive on that road all the way to my house."

"I can see why."

"The road was fine until the council decided it needed to be maintained. It's been like that for six years. Before that it was flat and smooth." He used his hand to show me what he meant, slowly sailing it horizontally through the air. "Then it snowed and they plowed and it's been like that ever since."

I bent low to examine the underside of my truck, checking the transfer case for leaking, wishing I had a skid-plate.

"Yeah, they maintain the hell out of it. Is everything okay under there?"

I got up. "Yeah, I think so."

"Well, when you leave, just take the other road." He pointed to a long straight lane from his house leading toward the highway.

"I didn't even see that at the highway," I said.

"No, I try to hide it up there. I've got some brush wired to the ground so that nobody will see it. Only a few people know about it, so keep it to yourself."

"Why?"

"So the tribal council won't come and maintain it. You see what they did to this road."

What he said sounded reasonable. I observed the admirable flatness of his private driveway and said, "Big Junior said you wanted to see me tonight. But I was over here now and thought I'd stop by."

"Come in."

I followed him through the door. "Have you seen Louise Yellow Calf lately?" I asked.

He gestured for me to sit in one of two rockers in front of his stoked and doorless potbellied stove. He sat in the other. The house was dim: the only light came from a single bulb suspended on a cord from the ceiling. The floor was of tired and cracked planks, gray and black in places. There was a photo of a man in uniform on the wall over a sofa that was covered with laundry. Hiram watched me without speaking for a full minute, then looked at his fire.

"Louise Yellow Calf is a little woman," he said.

"Yes."

"How do you know her?"

"I gave her a ride one day. I helped her take her mother to the hospital."

He nodded.

"You know about the FBIs who were killed," I said.

He nodded again.

I looked up at the photo over the sofa.

"That's my son," Hiram said. "He was killed by Korea."

"I'm sorry."

"He was a brave warrior. He died in," Hiram looked at the ceiling, "1966."

"Hiram, the Korean War was over by then. In '66 it was Vietnam."

"I know," he said.

"So, your son died in Vietnam?"

"No, he died in Rivertown."

"You said he was killed in Korea."

Hiram looked me in the eyes. "I said he was killed by Korea. The white army and killing those people." He shook his head. "They look like us, you know. My son, Bertram, was never the same. He came back and got drunk every night. His nose got big and red and he begged for rides into town. He froze to death one night. It was 1966. He was thirty-eight." He let my eyes go and looked back at the fire.

"I'm sorry," I said. "About the FBI men." I was trying to bring him back to the subject.

"I heard they got shot by the lake," he said.

"Louise showed up at my house that night, came in soaking wet and scared." I told him.

"I see." He rocked.

"I lied when I was asked if I knew Louise. I don't know why. I thought I was protecting her."

"It's a good thing, to protect people. We Indians are sick with the business of protecting people."

"I'm afraid I've implicated myself somehow."

Hiram nodded. Then he said, "I wanted to see you because I want to invite you into a meeting."

"What kind of meeting?"

"A meeting of the Native American Church."

"I'm not much on religion," I said.

"You don't have to be. I just wanted to invite you. The meeting is tonight. It's a peyote ceremony. But if you come you'll have to stay up until morning."

"I don't know. I mean, I feel honored. But why? You don't even know me."

"You drove Big Junior to the hospital and you didn't know him."

"That's not the same thing."

"You lied to protect Louise and you didn't know her."

"Maybe I'll come. Will it be here?"

"No, behind the Yellow Calf house."

"Okay. What time?"

"Eight. Nine."

"Okay." I looked at the flames of the fire. "Where is Louise?" I asked.

"I don't know. I think she left the reservation. I don't know where she went."

I stood up and, with my hand, stopped the rocker from moving. "Well, maybe I'll see you later."

We stepped outside and looked at the flow of the Plata through his front yard. The water seemed higher than it should have been for that time of year, almost covering the boulders in the flow. "You must get flooded out every year," I said.

"Never have been."

"But I heard that last year the little store had water in it." I looked across the flat at the ugly little building some five hundred yards away and scratched my head. "Didn't it flood up there?"

"It did, but I was dry as a bone."

I studied the lay of the ground and scratched my head. "Hiram, your house is lower than the store. You're not more than fifteen feet higher than the river here." I didn't believe what he was telling me, but I wasn't going to argue the matter. I realized that even if it wasn't true, he either understood flooding to be something other than I did or was trying to tell me something. I looked at the nearby cottonwoods and I couldn't see any signs of high-water marking—no lines, no wrinkled bark, nor did the ground around his house show any sign.

"The river goes where it wants to go," Hiram said. "So far, it hasn't wanted to come into my house."

.   .   .

The right to divert the unappropriated waters of any natural stream to beneficial uses shall never be denied. Priority of appropriation shall give the better right as between those using the water for the same purpose; but when the waters of any natural stream are not sufficient for the service of all those desiring the use of the same, those using the water for the domestic purposes shall have the preference over those claiming for any other purpose, and those using the water for agricultural purposes shall have preference over those using the same for manufacturing purposes.

.   .   .

While standing there talking to the old man I drifted to times with my grandfather, how he would tell me that trust was a thing best exercised sparingly. He didn't dislike white people, but he didn't trust them either. He told me about having seen a man lynched when he was thirteen, lynched by white men who talked about their god as if he were a neighbor, white men who made burnt offerings to him on cold Virginia nights. He didn't dislike Christians, but he didn't trust them either. He held firmly that his true beliefs were lost someplace inside him and inside his daughter and son and inside me, his only grandchild, and that the Christians had locked the door on those beliefs. He didn't dislike his wife for being a Christian, but he didn't trust her. For the same reason, he distrusted his daughter, even when she was a child. He left his wife, calling her a "tool" on his way out. His daughter and my grandmother accused him of thinking he was god. His daughter never called him when she grew up.

He took me hunting when I was ten and told me that if I ever started to be deceived by that "Jesus crap" that he would kick my ass. "That man I saw hanged," he said, "those Christians had cut off his testicles and stuck them in his mouth." He studied the reeds for signs or movement. "It's not their color, it's their god." Then he said, "And don't marry a Christian." He had deep-set, dark brown eyes and he said, as he reloaded, "They're sick. They believe in one way, their way." He fired at a duck and missed. "Your grandmother was a decent enough woman, but she was a sucker. Don't be a sucker, Robert." Years later my grandfather put the barrel of his over-and-under shotgun in his mouth and pushed the trigger with the tip of his cane.

Have you killed anyone?
How many have you murdered?
Have you eaten the flesh of man?
Have you eaten peyote?

.   .   .

The hidden, private drive of Hiram's was beautifully, remarkably smooth and a straight shot to the highway. Of course I wondered why Hiram had invited me into the ceremony and, of course, I kept coming back to the notion that somehow he wanted something from me. That thought made me nervous, but I was flattered as well as intrigued by the offer. I also felt at the time that, given my possible predicament with the FBI, I was not insistent enough when it came to answers about the whereabouts of little Louise Yellow Calf.

I drove back up the mountain. It was just after noon and the day was bright; the snow was throwing blinding refractions, twisting the light, torturing it. I wanted to understand its angles. When I walked into Clara's store I discovered Karen standing there helping her sort the jelly beans.

"Hello, Ugly," Clara said.

"Clara," I said and I walked past the two of them over to the refrigerator where I opened the door and grabbed a quart of milk. I felt sick and more than a little lost; the whole atmosphere of the place was transformed by Karen's presence. I walked back to the counter and put down my carton of milk.

"I'm sorry," Karen said.

"Yeah, well." I handed money over to Clara.

"I didn't know," Karen said.

"You never know."

Clara gave me my change.

"Please," Karen said. "How was I supposed to know she was an FBI agent?"

Clara was listening closely. She ate a red jelly bean, sliding it into her mouth as if watching a movie, cracking the outer surface of it with her teeth exposed.

"You weren't, Karen. You weren't supposed to know. You weren't supposed to be there. I'm not with you. I can fuck anybody I damn well please."

Karen was well rehearsed in point-missing and so she said, "So you *were* sleeping with her." Her body began that all-too-familiar trembling and she tapped her thigh through her thick coat.

"Even if I was, it's no business of yours. Please, just go back to Denver and drive somebody else crazy." The words felt good coming out and the hurt on her face didn't faze me. I could see all that was wrong with her and, more importantly, what was wrong with us. I picked up my carton of milk and walked slowly, deliberately out, not pausing to look back, not pausing to make out what her final, unintelligible sound meant.

I went back to my house and had a much-needed cup of tea. The irony of my stop at Clara's was that the milk turned out to be sour; it was swirling bad on top of the hot water. I collected a box of nymphs and my waders and marched through the woods to the creek, where I would be able to think, I hoped, more clearly. Really, what fishing did for me was to keep me from thinking. I was hypnotized by the water, the cast after cast into the flow, the riffles, the dips behind boulders where the

big fish were supposed to lie in wait for tumbling aquatic insect
larvae.

. . .

*The stream channel of Dog Canyon does not change significantly along
its length. The upper trench is extremely rough and rocky and then traverses across bedrock outcrops and flood plain deposits. The direction of
the flow alters abruptly numerous times as it comes to geologic forma-
tions and the results of differential erosion. These deposits become more
congested downstream and evidence of terraces emerges before the flood
plain widens.*

. . .

I tried again as I walked back to my cabin to understand the pre-
cipitous impulse that made me lie to protect Louise Yellow Calf.
My cheerless answer was not that it was in my nature, but that I
had a pathological disposition to know what was going on in all
matters, at all times, before I talked to anyone. I peered into myself and there, collecting in the bottom of the container like tur-
pentine or kerosene or some other useful but harmful substance,
was my urgent requirement to know. It was not a need to save
somebody, but simply a need to know. It was the same misaligned
need that had landed me in that relationship with Karen. I hadn't
wanted to help Karen become sane; rather I had wanted to know
what it was everyone meant when they said she was crazy. I hadn't
driven Special Agent Davies to my house instead of letting her
fend for her unconscious self in the restaurant in Rivertown because I wanted to help (although what else could I have done) but
because I had been curious about my own fear and loathing of her
as an FBI agent, and I had thought I might find out something. I
kicked myself all the way home. I knew that I would continue to
ask about Louise and that I wouldn't tell the FBI the truth. It was

not in me to volunteer information to the FBI. I might tell young Hanson, the deputy, but not the FBI.

. . .

. . .

Karen did not show up at my house, although I would not have been surprised to discover that she had been hiding in the woods watching my movements. At dusk I was getting ready to go down to Plata and into the ceremony with Hiram Kills Enemy. I wondered what it would be like, wondered if I should take the peyote if offered to me, wondered if anyone would tell me anything about Louise Yellow Calf.

It was snowing again.

. . .

The listing of peyote as a controlled substance in Schedule I does not apply to the nondrug use of peyote in bona fide *religious ceremonies of the Native American Church, and members of the Native American Church so using peyote are exempt from registration. Any person who manufactures peyote for or distributes peyote to the Native American Church, however, is required to obtain registration annually and to comply with all other requirements of the law.*

. . .

. . .

The drive through the snow was scary. The storm had worked itself up into a blizzard, a whiteout, and the road had become a sheet of ice. I thought that all I needed at that moment was to have Davies discover me on the reservation. I stopped at the little store by the flashing light again and bought a carton of generic cigarettes and a couple of cotton hand towels. I put a twenty-dollar bill into the seam of the cigarette box and was planning to offer it to Hiram as a kind of thank-you for the privilege of entering the meeting. I knew all too well the way to the Yellow Calf house, but as I couldn't see three feet in front of the truck, I drove by the house twice. I found the drive and discovered that my truck was the only vehicle there. I got out and walked around to the back. There was one man there, working beside the erected teepee. He was a tall man with two long braids falling down the back of his bright purple ski jacket. He gave me a weak wave and continued stacking wood beside the tent.

"My name is Robert," I said.

"Billy," he said.

"Hiram asked me to come to a meeting tonight," I said.

He groaned an acknowledgment and continued his task, making a very neat pile and keeping the wood covered with a green-and-blue plastic tarp. The snow was falling in huge flakes that kissed the tarp and disappeared.

"I must be really early," I said.

"No," Billy laughed. "You're on time. Everybody else is on Indian time."

I chuckled too. "We used to call it BPT, black people's time." I watched him for a minute. "Can I help you do that?"

He shook his head.

The wind whipped about like a rope of ice and I found myself ducking into the entry of the teepee to get away from it. "How long will it be?" I asked.

"Are you cold?" Billy asked.

"Yes," I said.

He looked at me for a long second. "I am, too."

"Do you know the Yellow Calf family?" I asked.

"Yes."

"Do you know Louise?"

"Yes."

"Have you seen Louise?"

"No."

"Do you know where she is?" I asked.

"Yes."

"Where is she?"

"Louise is in Los Angeles." He stood up from the tarp, having secured the edge of it to a stake with cord, and looked at me. "I don't know where in Los Angeles, but that's where she is."

"Do you know why she went there?"

"I suppose to do or find something she couldn't do or find here," Billy said. "Ain't that why people go places? You can help me now."

I followed him into the teepee. The inside was lit by a battery-powered lantern near the opening. There was no snow on the ground inside. Although we were out of the wind, the air was still plenty cold. "What do you want me to do?"

Billy grabbed the light and took it to the middle of the tent where he placed it on the ground. The white light shook our shadows against the walls of the tepee. He got down on his hands and knees and started examining the dirt, picking it up and letting it sift through his fingers. "Come down here," he said. "Look around and be sure there's no debris inside this center circle."

I then saw that a circle had been drawn in the ground with a stick or knife. I joined him in the middle of the teepee. "Debris?"

"Like this," he said and he held up a staple for me to see. "If it ain't dirt, it's debris."

I nodded and we worked our way from the center out to the edge of the circle. I found three nails, another six staples, a dime, and two pennies. Billy found a marble and a plastic eye from a child's doll, which he put into his pocket. I didn't ask him why.

It had been nearly an hour since my arrival. It was now nearly nine o'clock and still no one else had shown up. My feet were starting to feel numb from the cold. I was glad to have the information about Louise, but also dismayed that she had flown the coop on me, left me alone to face the police and the FBI and whatever sour music was going to be played.

Billy started with twigs, dry twigs that cracked in his fingers, then used sticks, then larger sticks as big around as his fleshy thumbs, and then small logs to construct the fire. He lit it deep in the middle, at the twigs, with a wooden match. The action of the flame was small at first, making it a little smoky inside the tent, the blaze low and orange. Then the sticks, in order, began to catch with crackling and shaking light that made me feel warmer although the actual heat had not yet found me. Billy kept the fireplace neat and immediately pulled away any ashes with a small broom, the kind found in the grocery store, straw wrapped with wire and a red handle. Soon the fire was hot, hot enough to push me away from it toward where my shadow found the tent wall. It was at this time that the others, with better sense than me, began to filter into the yard and the teepee.

Billy put his hand out to me. His face was sweating and he had shed his coat. I realized how hard he had been working. I shook his hand and he said, "Thank you."

"You're welcome. And thank you for telling me about Louise."

He nodded.

.   .   .

My grandfather had Parkinson's disease in his later years; his voice shook, and one day he sat on his testicles and hurt himself badly. He couldn't hunt so often anymore, the shaking of his hands was pronounced enough to ruin his aim, but he claimed not to feel a sense of loss. Once when he snapped awake from a nap as I was sitting beside him in the den of his house I thought I saw fear in his eyes, and looked at his hand trembling against the leather arm-rest. But later, when my aunt was visiting and trying to get him to try some soup she had made, telling him how they had lost so much time not talking over the years, she mentioned god and his eyes narrowed. Without batting an eye he said, "Give me hell and a glass of lemonade." He scared her right out of the house and right then, in that moment, I saw my grandfather as the most pro-foundly spiritual person I had ever met in my life. My father didn't care. He was, as I came to be, uncaring, thinking if he didn't know whether there's a god, then he simply didn't know. Why worry? Why care? But my grandfather was a true believer.

.   .   .

Feeling a little shy and a lot awkward, I found myself waiting in the cold for Hiram as men came into the tent. A couple of Plata introduced themselves to me and paused to chat briefly, but most just nodded amiably and walked on by. I liked that. Finally Hiram showed up.

He said, "Let's get inside. It's too cold out here."

A circle formed around the fire, around the wall of the teepee, stopping a few feet from either side of the entrance. The fire felt good. I took off my coat and sat on it to separate my ass from the cold ground. When Hiram seemed to break off from a conversation on his other side I said, "Hiram, these aren't my ways. Do you think I should take the medicine?"

He looked at the fire, his eyes already a little glazed, and said, "I have seen many miracles taking the medicine."

I thought, of course, you've been taking hallucinogenic drugs. "So, you think I should?"

Hiram nodded. "Don't take a big handful, though."

"Okay."

Hiram seemed so much more serious now than he had the other times I had been near him. I would be lying if I said that he didn't frighten me just a little. He leaned over to me and pointed to the fire with an open hand. "The ground looks very nice," he said.

·   ·   ·

Billy sat by the door and was up frequently to tend the fire, adding wood and sweeping away ashes. Two young men shared a drum and sang. The drum was a skin stretched over a short, cast-iron kettle that was filled with water. The singers drank from the drum through the skin and struck it with a stick, pressing on the skin with their fingers to find the pitch they desired. The singing was repetitive, hypnotic, and beautiful. Much of the beauty was in the disposition of the singers and in the listeners' reception. The teepee became almost hot from the fire. There was an occasional breath of cold air when Billy had to leave and enter with more wood.

There were several items laid out between Hiram, who was "putting up" the meeting, and the fire circle. There was a wand made of eagle feathers, and tobacco, and the ground-up peyote in a jar, and a large tin pot of tea made from the peyote. The men took turns praying in Plata, occasionally offering some words of English—for my benefit, I believed. They welcomed me and then forgot me. The meeting was for Louise's mother I learned during a long prayer from Hiram. Between songs and prayers there was time to chat. The man on my left was old and very fat and it struck me that I had seen very few fat Indian men. His name was Elijah and he nodded his head when he talked.

"You are a friend of Hiram's?"

"Yes."

"Is this your first time in a meeting?" he asked me.

"Yes."

"Good," he said. He stared at the fire for a while. "I knew a lot of black men in the army. Do you have Indian blood?"

"I don't know. Supposedly my grandmother was half Lumbee, but I don't know." I looked at the dark red stone on the ring he wore. "Is that a birth stone?"

He shook his head. "No, it's just something I bought at the Trading Post."

"It looks like a garnet," I said.

"I guess," he said. "I like red."

"Do you know Louise Yellow Calf?" I asked.

He nodded and said, "Not very well. She was around for a while, but they say she went back to Chicago."

"I heard she went to Los Angeles."

Nodding, he said "I hadn't heard that. It could be true though. I don't know her very well."

The medicine came around and Hiram suggested that I take a modest amount from the jar and place it in the palm of my hand. I took less than I saw him take and I tossed it into my mouth as he did and passed the jar to Elijah. The taste was truly awful, horrendous, almost alarmingly so, deeply nasty, and it sent a shiver crawling through me. Unhappily, as it was a powder, it wedged in between my teeth and continued to explode in my mouth after the initial eating of it. The pot, more a bucket actually, of tea that had been made from the cactus came around and we drank from the dented tin ladle. The tea tasted as terrible as the powder, but at least it went by my tongue quickly and served to rinse my mouth.

I nodded to Hiram and felt dreadfully nervous. I didn't know what to expect. I could feel my heart racing, not from the drug but from anxiety. The thought of experiencing a vision was exotic to me, as I had, I imagined, a typical if naive fascination with the spiritual life of these people. I felt like a tourist, but guilty as I didn't want my curiosity to seem frivolous or vapid. I waited and waited, took the medicine twice more as it came around, and then I waited some more, listening to the songs, the prayers in Plata, the chatting in between, staring at the fire, hoping the dancing flames might trigger something in me, watching Billy rake away the ashes and rake away the sweat from his forehead. Nothing happened. No sound, nor light, nor shadow became altered in my perception. The east-facing door began to show glimpses of the breaking morning as Billy collected more wood. I experienced no vision, saw no little coyote drive by the fire in a tiny station wagon, saw nothing but the morning come and felt nothing except for the numbing of my butt and the stiffening of my legs from having sat so long.

. . .

Contained in the inferior occipital fossae and stationed beneath the occipital lobes of the cerebrum and separated from it by the tentorium cerebelli is the cerebellum. It is flattened from the top down and is oblong, measuring 3.5 to 4 inches transversely and about 2 inches in the center. It is made up of gray and white matter, the gray matter here being darker than in the cerebrum and occupying the surface. The white matter is inside. Unlike the cerebrum, the surface of the cerebellum is not convoluted, but etched with many curved troughs or solci, varying in depth.

.   .   .

When the sun was up we filtered out into the light through the new deep blanket of snow. We waded, up to our knees, across the yard, stomping our boots on the back porch, and entered the Yellow Calf house where Mary Brown and some other women had food waiting. Mary Brown smiled at me. Her eyes were soft and I trusted them.

I nodded hello to her. "How are you?" I asked.

"I am good," she said.

"How is your sister?" I asked.

"She's in the hospital again."

I had already learned that in the meeting.

"How about you?" Mary Brown asked.

"I've been better." I looked at the plate of food she had handed me. Chokecherry gravy, fried bread, and dried meat. "I'd really like to find Louise," I said.

"I don't know where she went," Mary Brown said.

"Someone told me she went to Los Angeles and then someone else told me Chicago."

The woman looked about as if to see if anyone was listening and then whispered, not terribly softly, "She has a cousin in Denver who works in the big post office, the one by the airport."

"Why are you telling me?"

"I want you to find her," she said and I could see the concern in her eyes.

I looked at my plate and then out the window.

"You must find her," she said. "She's getting into trouble. I worry about her."

"Ms. Brown, I'm sorry, but I don't really know Louise. I just want to ask her a couple of questions."

Mary Brown touched my arm. Her touch was soft, but insistent. Her hand said please.

"I'll see if I can find her," I said.

Mary Brown nodded. "Louise didn't grow up here. She doesn't know."

"Doesn't know what?" I asked.

"Doesn't know."

"I'll try," I said. At least a trip to Denver to find Louise was far more reasonable and likely to be successful than either a trip to Chicago or Los Angeles. I was moved and frightened by the trust in me Mary Brown was showing. I studied the old woman's face and her unwavering eyes, and I knew right then that I was being manipulated by a pro. She had me. "What's the cousin's name?" I asked.

"Florence St. John."

I sat and ate, listening to bits of conversation, about the high-school basketball team, about the tribal council, about how the ranchers wanted to take the water, about how someone named Riverfish had stolen artifacts from a cultural center and stuck them into his archive at the mission, about how one word could make five hundred Indians say *shit* and that word was *bingo*. I then stepped outside, hoping to find Hiram before I left. He was standing by my truck.

"Leaving?" he asked.

"Yes," I said. "I ought to go check on my house and make sure the snow is on the roof and not the floor."

He smiled.

"Hiram, may I ask you something?"

"Of course."

"In the meeting, I took the medicine three times. But nothing happened. Why? Is that normal? Nothing changed in what I saw or heard."

He looked at the ground by my truck as if to check my tires, then said, "How do you know?"

"I guess I don't," I laughed softly and opened my door. "I'll see you later."

"See you later," he said.

I drove slowly over the terrible roads, which were not as bad as the night before simply because I could see where I was going, north and toward the big mountain. I wondered if Davies or Karen were waiting for me at my cabin.

. . .

Hell-hole Creek is wider than Dog and Skinner Canyons. The sides of Hell-hole Canyon are only moderately steep, thus providing a more expansive bare surface area for runoff generation. Here, as in Dog Canyon, bedrock outcroppings exert influence on the disposition of terraces, ledges, and soils and affect markedly the lateral and vertical migration of the stream trough.

The stream bed of Hell-hole Creek traverses bedrock and alluvial matter. It is contained within a wide flood plain. High-water marks and flood debris were observed with widths as much as 125 feet. Three terraces are distinctly visible.

Flow was estimated using standard equations approximately seven miles from the confluence with Plata Creek. There the creek was cut into lime and mudstone. Flow values ranged from 1,300 to 2,700 cubic feet per second. (See attached calculations.)

. . .

When we speak of the education of the Indians, we mean that comprehensive system of training and instruction that will convert them into American citizens, put within their reach the blessings that the rest of us enjoy, and enable them to compete successfully with the white man on his ground and with his own methods. Education is to be the medium through which the rising generations of Indians are to be brought into the fraternal and harmonious relationship with their fellow citizens, and with them enjoy the sweets of refined homes, the delight of social intercourse, the emoluments of commerce and trade, the advantages of travel, together with the pleasures that come from literature, science, and philosophy, and the solace and stimulus afforded by a true religion.

· · ·

When I arrived at my cabin I found a note crammed into the crack between the knob and jamb. It was from Karen and I didn't bother to read whatever was written above her name. I unlocked the door and walked inside, stuffed the note into the cold stove, making certain the ashes smothered it, and sat down in the big chair. Glancing over at my tying table I saw that it was beginning to collect dust; the tail feathers sticking high out of the big jar were especially dusty. What I really wanted to do right then was go fishing, but I knew I wouldn't. Although I was sitting there without a fire I didn't want to be cold at that moment, I didn't want to be uncomfortable, so I got up, grabbed my duffle from the closet and tossed some clothes into it, underwear and socks mostly, as I had clothes already at my place in Denver.

6

My father said he didn't want me to be in the house alone. That was why he woke me to make the drive with him way out to Hopper in the middle of the night so he could see a patient. I was groggy, still a little asleep, I think, as somehow I ended up dressed and sitting in the cold car beside him. We drove out of the city and into the swallowing blackness of the countryside. It seemed so dark out there, so empty and scary, and I remembered all those stories about cars with dead headlights coming up silently behind black people at night. We rolled on for about forty minutes as the heat in the car finally blew too hot to be comfortable. We pulled up to a long, narrow house set on short pillars of brick. I could see under the dwelling as our headlights' beams swung across the yard when we crunched to a stop on the gravel. There were lights on in the windows and I could see heads moving about the rooms. My father and I walked up the steps onto the porch. I remember being frightened by a dog lying beside the steps, although the animal didn't move, just followed us with his droopy eyes. A woman screamed inside.

A tall, lean man let us in. He had a snaggle-toothed grin and very large hands. He almost bowed to my father and called him "Doc Hawks." My father pointed me over toward the sofa without saying anything and was then met by an old woman with a yellow scarf tied about her head.

"You've got a problem, Ms. Jenkins?" my father said.

"It's too much for me," the woman said, shaking her head.

Whoever was in trouble screamed again and my skin crawled

and I huddled into the corner of the sofa, staring at the fire behind the black slats of the potbellied stove. The man who had let us in sat in a bentwood rocking chair closer to the heat. My father disappeared into the back of the house. I watched the man rock, a slow rhythm, and after every five or six rocks he'd come up to his mouth with a bottle he held down on the floor and take a swig. I could smell him, a sourness. The woman howled again.

I had to pee. I tried to wiggle around on the sofa to make the urge pass, but it wouldn't and I realized that I'd had to go since before we had left our house. I wanted to ask the man where the bathroom was, but I was frightened by his trance, the way he just stared at the fire, rocking like that, and scared by the way he smelled. I got up and he didn't seem to notice, at least he didn't acknowledge my movement. I walked outside. I didn't want to pee in anyone's front yard, it didn't seem right and I was too shy to run the risk of discovery. I walked around to the side and found that the lazy dog was walking with me; his old bones were still stiff from sleep so he was limping. I touched his head, which he didn't seem to mind, as he showed no reaction, but simply kept up with my pace. I relieved myself close to the house and I heard another scream. I looked through the closest window.

I couldn't see much. I saw my father's back and the woman with the yellow scarf standing off in the corner in front of an open closet; she was holding a fat Bible to her chest. I could just make out the top of the woman's head. She was lying in the bed and I could see her brown knees. I saw her open mouth when she threw back her head to scream. Then I saw my father holding something limp in his hands, something wet, something important, and I saw the lips of the woman in the yellow scarf moving like crazy. My father worked over the thing for long minutes, his back to me, although from his motions I knew the look on his face, could feel it, and I forgot about being cold and watched as he finally stood and just shook his head. The woman in the bed cried and the woman with the Bible ran to comfort her.

I was back on the sofa when my father came into the room. The man in the rocker was passed out, the tips of his long fingers barely touching the mouth of the brown-paper-wrapped bottle. We didn't say anything, just got into the car and left. Once on the dark road with the heat blowing hard and dry from the vents, I said, "So, the baby died."

My father nodded, sighed, and looked over at me; he seemed a little surprised.

.   .   .

The drive to Denver was three hours long, over bad roads, through bad weather. Conditions in Denver always seemed extreme, never drizzling but flooding, never a dusting of snow or flurries but blizzards and sheets of ice, hail, tornadoes. The Karen of cities. That day the sky was a sick yellow-gray, the face of the fallen snow was scarred by pollution, and the highway was messy with traffic-dirty slush and ice. I got off the freeway and drove through downtown to escape a traffic jam. I stopped in at a little coffee shop on Larimer Square for a bite and to readjust to the atmosphere. I sat at a little table in the back and was waited on by a young woman in a way-too-short skirt and a mod haircut. I asked what kind of muffins they had and she ran down an impressive list with equally impressive speed. Finally I stopped her and asked for a simple bran muffin, to which she responded, "Bran crunch, bran flake, honey bran, bran and apple, or healthy bran?"

"Healthy bran? What are the others? Are they dangerously high in fiber?"

She popped her gum and looked across the room, waiting for me to finish my order.

"Healthy bran," I said, "and a Coke."

.   .   .

In accordance with normal procedures followed when an unidentified
body is found on the reservation, an autopsy was requested by the BIA.
No agents of the FBI were present when the autopsy was performed, but
SA Gearing, SA William Wird and SA Daniel Price viewed the body
at the PHS Hospital, Sharp Corners, CO, prior to the autopsy, and SA
Richard Mums viewed the body after the autopsy. The autopsy was per-
formed by R. B. Mitchell, Alliance, NE, who stated in his initial report
that the probable cause of death was exposure.

. . .

The healthy bran muffin turned out to be the sweetest thing I had
ever eaten in my life and my head was still reeling from it when I
walked into my apartment. I opened the blinds and looked over at
the telephone answering machine, which I had inexplicably forgotten to turn off, and saw it flashing. I sat and pressed the play
button while I tried to recall living there. There were many messages from Karen that consisted of open air and then a click; a
message from a new guy named Ted at the Naturalists' Conservancy asking if I could come back to work early; a message from
Special Agent Gladys Davies asking me to call; and finally a spoken missive from Karen. "Robert, so I made a fool of myself once
again and I continue to do so by calling you once more. There are
just so many things I want to say, but I know I've already said
them. What did I do? What didn't I do? Why don't you care for
me the way I care for you? You make me so mad . . . I hate . . .
I love you, Robert. Please call me. I'm about to come undone.
Robert? Robert? Are you there listening as I'm leaving this message? *Robert?*"

. . .

I had met Karen three years earlier, but it was not until one year
earlier that I first went out with her. She was working at a photo

lab that was trying to become an advertising agency, which no doubt was the reason they had done such a poor job developing the aerial photos I had left with them and was why I was in the office complaining.

"These are for work," I said to the pony-tailed man. "These are not art shots. I have to be able to read these."

"I don't see what the problem is," he said.

I took another photo from my case. "Look, this is a good print. See here. That's a creek. Now, look at this piece of shit." I put his work in front of him. "Somewhere in this mess is a river. Would you show it to me?"

"I can't change the negative," he said.

"They're from the same fucking negative," I snapped. "I just had this one done down the street at the one-hour place."

"What's your point?" he asked.

"I'd like my money back."

He started to say something, but was cut off by a woman who was standing in the doorway behind him. "Give him his money," she said, calmly.

"But Karen, you know what Rod said," the man with the pony tail whined.

"Give it to him."

The man gave me my money and I thanked the woman who turned out to be Karen, someone I'd met two years before, who turned out to be a good friend of the wife of one of my fishing buddies, and who turned out to be free for dinner. The dinner went well enough, full of pleasant chatter and like-minded political mindlessness, and I dropped her off thinking that she was nice enough and that I wouldn't object to seeing her again. The next day the wife of my fishing buddy, who had learned from Karen of our date, called me and warned me off. Ellen said, "I've always liked you, Robert, so I'm telling you this straight out. Karen is totally crazy."

"What are you saying?" I asked.

"She's crazy. She's obsessive, neurotic, psychotic. You name it. Do yourself a favor and stay away from her. I'm not joking, Robert. I'm not exaggerating."

"You're her friend."

"I'm her only friend."

"She seemed fine to me," I said.

"Yeah, that's how she seems. I've watched her for years. Just trust me on this."

"It doesn't sound fair to call somebody crazy. Maybe she's just intense, different." I knew how stupid it sounded when I was saying it, but having said it, I decided to stand by it.

"Call it what you want. But don't come back later saying I didn't warn you."

I hung up, with a weird resolve to decide for myself who was crazy and who wasn't. The more I thought about Ellen calling Karen crazy, the more I wanted, perhaps irrationally, to defend her. And I didn't even know her. That was really crazy. And so the crazy man took out the allegedly crazy woman two more times; the third time ended up in my bed. We fucked the many times standard for first-time fucking and talked the usual way about how well we got along.

"What are you doing for Thanksgiving?" she asked, looking up from nuzzling my penis with her nose.

"No plans," I said.

"How about driving down to Santa Fe with me to visit with my parents?"

"I don't know," I said. I felt rushed.

She pretended to bite my penis. "Say, yes," she giggled. "Say, yes. Say, yes."

I said, "Yes."

. . .

$Qs \simeq b\lambda S/d,p$ *where* Qs *is the bed matter load moved through channels with equivalent water discharge,* b *is width,* λ *is wavelength,* S *is slope,* d *is sediment size, and* p *is sinuosity.*

.   .   .

I left my apartment after some brief and unsatisfactory rest and went to visit my friends Hal and Ellen. I was hoping to forget about the business on the mountain and get a free meal.

Ellen and Hal always ate soup for dinner. I sat at their table staring at my bowl and trying not to fall asleep. I looked up to find the two of them studying me closely. Although Ellen was close to and no doubt in touch with Karen, I had hoped she would have the good judgment or at least the decency to not to bring up her name.

"I talked to Karen," Ellen said. "So, we needn't discuss any of that. Suffice it to say, I told you so."

I nodded, appropriately cowed.

"We heard about the FBI men up there," Hal said. "Pretty nasty business."

"It happened on my side of the lake."

"You're kidding?" Hal said.

I shook my head and slurped down a spoonful of soup. It was some kind of cold soup that went down thickly, catching in my throat, and was more unsatisfying with each spoonful. "I had to talk to all sorts of cops and FBI people."

"Ah, so we heard," Ellen said and it sounded loaded the way she said it.

"What did you hear?" I asked.

"Karen told me she caught you in bed with some inspector from the FBI," Ellen said, wiping her mouth.

"Karen is a nut."

Ellen and Hal nodded.

"She's not going to let go yet," Ellen said.

Hal caught my eyes and said, "So, how is the fishing up there?" He salted his soup for a third time.

"Not bad. The water's pretty good."

Ellen cleared her throat. "You never should have slept with her in the first place."

"You're absolutely right, Ellen," I said.

"And you certainly shouldn't have gone with her to visit her parents." She slurped down a spoonful of soup. "That was the kiss of death. To meet her parents. Hell, *I've* never met her parents."

"Did you sleep with the FBI woman?" Hal asked.

"No."

"What was she doing in your shower?"

"Getting clean, I suppose. Or counting her bullets. I don't know. I don't care. Listen, she was some kind of kook who got drunk and passed out and I didn't know what to do with her." It sounded really bad as I said it. "Anyway, nothing happened."

"Man," Hal muttered.

"You shouldn't have slept with her," Ellen said again.

.   .   .

The next morning, after a rough night—the soup had affected me badly—I called the big post office, the one out by the airport, the one where people went deaf from the machines and the employees had to walk through metal detectors ever since a disgruntled class-D zipcode sort assistant step II went berserk with an AK converted to full automatic. "Used to be a nice place to work," a twenty-year postal worker shouted at the television camera responding to the question "Did you see it happen?" After twenty minutes the hesitant and cautious voice of Florence St. John was on the other end.

"Ms. St. John?"

"Yes?"

"My name is Robert Hawks and I'm a friend of your cousin, Louise Yellow Calf."

"Yes?"

"Well, I'm trying to find Louise," I said.

"There's no Louise here," she said and hung up, sharply.

So I drove out to the large post-office building. It wasn't the post office, I discovered, but some kind of regional office or distribution center and so there really wasn't a place for customers, but I found a small section set aside for visitors to park their cars. Then I entered through one door and then another until I was standing at a window talking to a fat man.

"I'm looking for a woman who works here by the name of Florence St. John," I said.

"What section does she work in?" he asked. He was laboring over a big ham-and-cheese sandwich with mayonnaise oozing from its edges.

"I don't know. I called earlier and whomever I was talking to was able to find her."

"And you're implying that I ain't able to find her, is that it?" the fat man said.

"I didn't say that."

"You might as well have said it."

"Florence St. John," I repeated the name.

"I can find anybody in this fucking place," he said, wiping mayonnaise from his mouth with a paper napkin and looking at it before he put it down beside his sandwich. "I know my damn business," he groaned as he grabbed a clipboard from under his phone. "Nobody in this damn place can find people the way I can find people. And it sure as hell ain't that bastard Johnson. He don't know shit, telling me I ain't got no merit increase coming. What was that name?"

"Florence St. John."

"Damn right. Nobody can't find a sum-bitch in this fucking place the way I can." He picked up the phone. "Leroy, you got a Frances St. John working over there? No? Well, fuck you, too." He hung up. "Fucking bastard." He studied the clipboard and picked up the phone again. "You got a Frances St. John over there."

"Florence," I said softly, but he didn't hear me.

"Yeah," he said into the phone. "Florence, yeah, that's the one. What's your section number? Q-9? Thanks." He hung up and looked at me. "Q-9."

"Where's that?"

"How the fuck should I know?" He buzzed the door unlocked and nodded for me to use it. "Just ask back there. You'll find it." As I passed through the door into the corridor I could still hear him. "Fucking bastards, every one of them."

I followed the corridor to a door that led outside, followed a sidewalk to another building, and entered. I stopped a smiling man and asked if he could tell me where Q-9 was.

"Building Q is two buildings over, through this building and out and it's the next one."

"Thanks."

I found building Q, and when I opened the door I was struck with an enormous and frightening wall of noise—roaring low groans, staccato chirps, and a constant high-pitched whining. The outside door opened into a huge open warehouse, filled with machines and exposed girders, hanging wires, people driving carts, people driving forklifts, and everyone wearing ear protection, huge yellow muffs with eagles painted on the sides. I walked to a man near me who was standing by a rapidly moving conveyer watching letters and packages go by.

"Excuse me!" I shouted, but he didn't hear me. I tapped his shoulder and he turned to face me. His eyes were red and tired looking. "Excuse me," I said.

"What!?"

"Excuse me!" I looked behind him and saw all that mail zipping by on the black pad of the conveyer while he wasn't watching. He didn't switch the machine off. He didn't glance back. "I'm trying to find somebody!"

"What!?"

"Florence St. John! Flo-rence Saint-John!" The passing mail made me feel nervous, anxious, agitated.

"Florence?!" he asked.

I nodded.

He pointed with his thumb to the near corner where a tall woman was sitting on a high stool tossing mail into several bins. She was finishing a handful of letters as I approached, and although I didn't think she saw me, she got up and headed for the exit door behind her. I trotted and caught the door before it could swing completely shut. I walked behind her, glad to be out of the din of the big room. Her ear protectors were around her neck like a choker. The women's rest room was another several steps away from her.

"Florence," I said.

She turned around and looked at me suspiciously, her brown eyes narrow, her arms tense, her hands forming into fists at her sides, not combatively but in a manner of withdrawal.

"I'm Robert Hawks. I'm a friend of Louise."

Florence St. John looked up past me to the door and then behind herself down the corridor.

"I called earlier. Mary Brown wants me to contact Louise." I looked at her eyes, tried to hold them, tried to have her trust me. "Mary Brown told me she was here in Denver with you."

"She told you wrong. I haven't seen Louise in a long time. Last I heard she was in Seattle."

"Mary Brown wants her to call home," I said.

She looked at me as if I were an enemy. "I don't know where Louise is, but if she calls me I'll give her the message."

I nodded.

She turned and entered the rest room.

"I really am a friend of hers," I said as the door closed.

Article 15. A primary object of this instrument being to advance the interests and welfare of the Plata people, it is agreed that, if it prove insufficient to effect these ends from causes that cannot be foreseen, Congress may hereafter make such further provision, by law, not inconsistent herewith, as experience may prove to be necessary to promote the interests, peace, and happiness of the Plata people.

. . .

The rain was letting up as I stared ahead through the windshield of my grandfather's Buick. The water came in frequent enough drops that he left on the wipers but they were infrequent enough that they made an awful noise against the glass. I didn't know where we were going. My grandfather'd picked me up from school, the way he always did on Tuesdays: my father never allowed me to take the bus and certainly never to walk, ever since he had received threatening calls from rednecks expressing concern about my safety. I found out about the calls some years later; at the time I was simply confused and a bit put out by what I considered irrational, overprotective behavior.

"Where are we going?" I asked my grandfather.

"I've got to make a house call."

I nodded. I was used to it.

We drove over to Reynolds Road, a section of town that was talked about as being bad. The houses were smaller and there seemed to be more clotheslines, but that was all the difference I could make out. We parked in front of a one-story house with a screened porch, and my grandfather said, "You'd better come in with me."

I followed him to the door and it opened. We were let in by a woman with a large Afro who, after we had passed, remained by the door, peeking out through the curtains. The house smelled like our attic, stale and dusty, and I smelled a stale beer that was sitting half drunk in a glass on the counter next to me. I followed my grandfather into the next room where a man and two women were attending to a man who was covered with blood. There was blood on the floor and blood all over the cushions of the chair on which the injured man sat. The man's chest was bare and I could see that the hands helping him were trying to stop the flow of blood from the hole just above his right nipple. The wounded man was fairly conscious, muttering and groaning.

"Get him up here on this table," my grandfather said.

The two women, the man, and my grandfather lifted the bloody man and put him up there on his back. His left shoe fell off, and for some reason I picked it up and held it for him. It was a big black shoe like the ones bus drivers wore, with new leather laces. My grandfather leaned in and examined the wound, peeling through the layers of towels that had been applied. One of the women looked at me and offered a slight and nervous although friendly smile.

"He's lost a lot of blood," my grandfather said.

"Fucking pigs," the standing man said. "He wasn't doing shit and them pigs shot him. All he was doing was delivering sand-wiches to the shelter. Delivering sandwiches."

"He's going to be all right, isn't he?" the woman who had smiled at me asked.

"He's lost a lot of blood."

"We can't take him to the hospital," the man said. "They'll come get him and they'll kill him. You know it. They'll take him to jail and let him bleed to death."

My grandfather was so much older than these people. He was wearing his usual herringbone jacket and his striped tie and they were dressed in fatigues with bandanas tied around legs or heads.

"Bring me a big pot of boiling water and some clean towels or rags," my grandfather said.

Blood was dripping off the table and onto the floor. I backed up and was standing near the window.

"Hey, come away from there, little brother," the man said to me, indicating the window.

I liked the way he called me little brother, as if I weren't little.

My grandfather worked over the man, digging into his wound and pulling out the bullet as the man's body tightened in response to the pressure and pain of the extraction. Grandfather was bloody up to his elbows, and sighing frequently. Then, as he was closing the wound, the woman from the front room stepped in.

"Somebody's at the door," she said.

"Shit," the uninjured man said.

He pulled a pistol from his trouser pocket and stood quietly. The woman who had smiled picked up a pump-action shotgun with a shortened barrel from behind a bookcase. My grandfather looked at me, breathing hard, his age showing on his face. He was listening. We were all listening. The knocking came again. Then once more. Then there was nothing.

. . .

The drive down to Santa Fe was long and uneventful and I was feeling, much as Ellen had warned me I'd feel with Karen, pursued. We stopped in a couple of places to eat and she told me some things about her parents. Her father, James Reskin, was a born-again endocrinologist, the son of Jewish parents and an avid hunter of upland game. Edith, her mother, was a dyed-in-the-wool Democrat who had fantasies about FDR—and she was still a Jew.

"That's her last line in any argument with my father," Karen said, drinking from the red plastic water glass at our lunch stop in Trinidad. "'At least, I'm still a Jew,' she says." Karen smiled.

We arrived late that evening and I was surprised to find that we would be sharing a room and a bed. Certainly, I knew that they knew we slept together, but still. . . . And after small talk, of course Karen wanted to make love. I could think only about her mother and father in the room next door, but she wouldn't stop. She grabbed me and sucked me and so I made love to her with my hand cupped over her mouth, which served only to excite her more. She screamed into my hand and the bed banged against the wall. I imagined Dr. Reskin on his knees praying for all of us.

The following morning, after a fitful sleep, I awoke to the sound of movement in the room and I rolled over to see Dr. Reskin standing before the window and a day that had not yet begun. He was holding a broken-down shotgun. I reached beside me in bed for Karen and didn't find her. Reskin engaged the barrels with a clack and looked at me.

"Good morning?" I said.

"You ever hunt turkey?" asked Reskin.

"Once," I said. "With my grandfather."

"The turkey is a good, big bird. A wise and clever bird. You can hunt a band of turkeys for a week and never see one. *Meleagris gallapavo.*" He turned to face the window and looked out. "Quite an animal."

"Yes, sir."

"Well, get up and put on some clothes and we'll see if we can't bag us one."

"Do I have time to shower?"

He frowned. "No."

I sat up, less concerned now for my immediate welfare, and rubbed my eyes and the back of my neck. "What if we don't get one?"

"We've got a Butterball in the freezer. We'll put the bastard in that fucking convection oven down there and that'll be it. Besides, wild turkeys are cunning, few and far between. You must know that. Can't count on them."

"Okay, I'll get dressed."

"All right then. I'll be downstairs waiting." With that, he left. His heavy boots marked time across the floor and then down the hallway outside.

I pulled on my jeans, laced up my boots, grabbed a silk undershirt from my bag, and put on a flannel shirt over that. I washed my face and stared at it in the mirror; I felt lost and sad. Downstairs in the kitchen I found Karen and her mother, in cozy robes, sitting at the table having coffee. I joined them.

Reskin came stomping in from outside. "Gear's all packed," he said.

"Don't we need a dog?" I asked.

He laughed. "Hell, you know that turkey is still hunting." He bent and kissed his wife's forehead and then Karen's. "We're off." Privately, I agreed.

Karen and Edith waved from the driveway as we rolled away in the doctor's old International Scout. There was little traffic in Santa Fe on that Thanksgiving morning. We drove north out of town, then east, off the highway and along a dirt road higher into the mountains, and then stopped at a clearing. I stood at the back of the truck while Reskin took the shotguns from the rack, draped a shell-sack over his shoulder, and then handed one to me.

"I've seen turkeys up here before," he said.

The shotgun he'd put into my hands felt familiar, like the one my grandfather had, the one he let me fire when I was twelve and the recoil put me on my butt.

"Here, put this on." He handed me a bright orange skullcap and pulled one on himself. "Gotta know where the other is."

We walked out across the clearing, then into the trees. There was only a thin layer of snow and the ground showed through in many places. The sun was up and some of the chill was being taken out of the air.

"The turkey is some bird," Reskin said as we walked. "A noble creature. Benjamin Franklin wanted him as the national emblem." He stopped, knelt, studied the ground, then rose to walk on. "You've got to hunt him as you would a deer or elk. Find some sign and wait him out. That's all you can do." He stopped and pointed to a place where some ground had been scratched up. "There you go," he said. We stepped up the slope and he had me hunker down behind a juniper. "Now you just wait here and when you see one, pow, you let him have it." He scurried on up the trail to find a stand of his own.

The ground was cold and I tried to pull my jacket under my butt to keep the seat of my trousers dry. The sky was bright blue, almost cheery, and I was hating being there. I looked around and yawned, then I fell asleep.

I sprang to my feet at the sound of a shot and grabbed the gun. I followed the direction Reskin had taken and some seventy yards up the trail I found him leaning against a spindly aspen. He was visibly shaken. He held his shotgun by the barrel, the stock hung at his shin.

"What is it?" I asked.

"I shot him," he whispered.

The way he was talking I assumed quickly that he was talking about a person, somebody, and I said, nervously, "Who did you shoot? Another hunter?"

"No, a turkey." He looked at me strangely, his eyes weak and sad, his mouth loose, and said, "I hid him over there."

I looked and saw nothing. "Where?"

"Over here." He walked over and pulled up some brush and there on bare, snowless ground was a good-sized tom, sprawled awkwardly and lifeless, one wing spread out over the head and the tail fanned out as if in display.

"Why did you hide him?" I asked.

"He's so large," Reskin said. "He's just so damn big."

.   .   .

The Bureau is considering the feasibility of instituting a program of disruption to be directed against organizations which seek to mobilize and effect a "political awareness" among blacks and Indians. . . . In considering this matter, you should bear in mind that the Bureau desires to disrupt the activities of these organizations and is not interested in mere harassment.

.   .   .

The phone was ringing as I entered my apartment. I watched it as I crossed the room. I was afraid it would turn out to be Karen and more afraid that it would be Davies. The machine would answer it in another two rings. I picked up the receiver.

"Robert?"

I recognized the small voice.

"So you're here."

"Stop trying to find me," Louise said.

"Mary Brown wanted me to find you. I think she's afraid your mother is dying."

"Give up."

"I'll just go back to the post office and bother your cousin Florence again."

"Give up."

"What's going on?" When she said nothing I considered the

possibility that the phone was tapped. "Okay, I understand. Um, well, I'll see you around. What shall I tell Mary Brown?"

"Tell her I'm all right," Louise said.

"Yeah, it's a real zoo up there," I said. "She said Hiram is going to treat your mother tomorrow at four. Hiram's in the house setting up. Yep, it's a real zoo up there."

There was another silence.

"Okay, then, I'll tell her you're all right."

I hung up the phone and my hands were shaking. I believed she understood my message, but I didn't know if she would comply.

. . .

Later that evening, I stupidly went to a place I had often gone for dinner. I went there as though I knew what I was doing, as though I wanted to see someone I might know, even though that was the last thing I wanted. I wanted to lie low, but because there was no food in the house and because I found myself too brain-dead to think of another place to go, I went there. So I walked into the restaurant and there was Karen. She was sitting at a table in the front as if I had called and asked her to meet me there. She was with a man and I was happy to see this, but before I could turn around and escape unseen, she spotted me. I let the hostess seat me, regrettably at a table only twenty feet from Karen and her date. I read over the menu, and tried to avoid her constant stare. I could peripherally see that her companion was twisting to see just what was commanding so much of her attention. Then she got up and walked over to me.

"So," she said, "you're back in town."

I didn't say anything, but tried instead to become as small and invisible as possible.

Too loudly, she said, "Where's your FBI honey?"

"I don't have anything to say to you, Karen. You're being awfully rude to your friend."

Loudly again, "He's no friend, just some guy."

"Some guy" got up, put his napkin on the table, and left the restaurant, a move I found worthy of mimicking, so I got up, too. That's when Karen fainted. People at nearby tables gasped as she swooned and fell into me. Reflexively, I caught her and brought her gently to the floor. Diners left their tables and huddled around us, their faces open and craning on long necks, their voices garbled and constant. I dipped my fingers in my water glass and dripped a little on her face, shook her a little.

Karen's eyes opened, she looked at me, and said, with all those people there, "You slept with her, didn't you?"

I felt the bystanders looking at me, penetrating my worn-thin veneer, moralizing, and trying to commit my sorry face to memory for later warnings to daughters and friends.

"Madam," I said, "I'm afraid you have me confused with someone else." I let her head rest on the floor and stood up. "She'll be all right," I said, authoritatively, then stepped backward through the crowd and left the building.

.   .   .

Edith Reskin balked at the prospect of plucking the turkey, but a stern look from Reskin sent her stomping to the sink with the carcass. She was cursing him and saying, "The man is a lunatic, a New Testament–thumping lunatic."

This was the first time in twelve years of Thanksgiving Day hunts that the good doctor had returned with a kill. An actual wild turkey had never really been expected. Reskin didn't know quite what to make of it. He was a little nervous and of the mind that I had brought him this good fortune. He sat silently in his study awaiting his turkey dinner. Karen was thrilled with the bird. She cornered me in the upstairs bathroom as I stepped from the shower. I grabbed her by the shoulders and looked her in the eyes.

"No," I said. "Not in this house."

"I want it," she said.

"Not in this house."

Her eyes grew moist and she ran down the hallway to the bedroom. I finished drying and followed her. She was stretched face down across the bed, crying.

"I'm sorry, Karen, but I simply don't like it. This is your parents' house. Their bedroom is right there for crying out loud. Your father has guns."

"That's beside the point."

"You're crazy," I said. "The fact that he has guns couldn't be more to the point."

"Don't you think they know we sleep together?"

"Now, that's beside the point. Listen, don't you want me to be comfortable?"

"Of course I do."

"Okay, then."

She was silent while I dressed. The tears ended and she sat up. "Do you ever think of marriage?" she asked.

I looked up from buttoning my shirt. "I guess."

"What about us?"

"Pardon?"

"Do you think we'll be together for a long time?"

My blood ran chilly through me and I felt my throat nervously clearing itself. "Karen, I don't know. We've really just met."

She looked hurt. "What are you saying?"

"We've got to know each other better. I mean, I'm looking forward to that, aren't you?"

"Promise me something," she said.

"What's that?"

"Promise I'll die first."

I tucked in my shirttail. "What are you talking about?"

"Promise me that I will die before you."

"What?"

"I don't think I could stand being left alone."

"Okay, you can die first. Let's go down to dinner."

. . .

Wukea-boo, his x mark
(Shaved Head) Chief Camanche

Wa-ya-ba-tos-a, his x mark
(White Eagle) chief of band

Hai-nick-seu, his x mark
(The Crow) chief of band

Paro-sa-wa-no, his x mark
(Ten Sticks) chief of band

Wa-ra-kon-alta, his x mark
(Poor Coyote Wolf) chief of band

Ka-na-re-tah, his x mark
(One that Rides the Clouds) chief of the southern Camanches

To-hau-sen, his x mark
(Little Mountain) Chief Kiowas

Si-tank-ki, his x mark
(Sitting Bear) war chief

Tah-ka-el-bool, his x mark
(The Bad Smelling Saddle) headman

Che-koon-ki, his x mark
(Black Horse) headman

On-ti-an-te, his x mark
(The Snow Flake) headman

El-bo-in-ki, his x mark
(Yellow Hair) headman

Si-tah-le, his x mark
(Poor Wolf) Chief Apache

Oh-ah-te-kah, his x mark
(Poor Bear) headman

Ah-zaah, his x mark
(Prairie Wolf) headman

Zootz-zah, his x mark
(The Cigar) headman

8

"I don't want him here," my grandfather said.

"Well, he's coming," my father said.

"Civil rights," my grandfather spat on the ground. He was leaning against the wall of the house, outside in the fenced yard in which we kept the dog. My father was examining the pear tree. I was petting the dog, an overweight German shepherd named Bertha. My father and grandfather often spoke out in the yard, since my grandfather claimed he felt safer there. "Nobody's going to give anybody any rights," Grandfather said. He looked at me. "Lies, nothing but lies," he said. "You're going to teach this boy lies. No such things as rights, Robert."

"Go on in the house, Rob," my father said. "We'll be inside in just a few minutes."

"You might as well tell him to believe in Santa Claus. Some white man coming down the chimney to give a black boy gifts. That's what's this rights talk is. Santa Claus. Let some white man land on our roof and see what happens."

"Go on inside," my father said, again.

I walked away toward the door, but I did so slowly.

"You're wrong, Papa," my father said, his voice sounding tired. "Things are changing. They're changing slowly, but they're changing. It's happening."

"Where?" My grandfather coughed. "I don't want that man here. It's that Christian bullshit that bothers me the most. Black people running around after some white man's invention."

"Whatever," my father said. "He's got people mobilized, that's all I know."

I sat on the steps of the back door and continued to listen.

My father cleared his throat. "A policeman came by the office today while you were out."

"Yes?"

"He asked me where I was last Thursday afternoon. Then he asked me where you were. I told him you were in the office with me. He asked me if I'd treated any gunshot wounds recently. I said no. I said no for both of us."

"What kind of cop?"

"FBI. At least, that's what he said."

"Did you ask him if it was any of his fucking business who I treated and where?"

"No, I didn't. Papa, I'm worried about Rob. And I'm worried about you."

"Yeah, I'm sorry, but he just happened to be with me. Son, I simply don't want to become more *watched* than we are now. And that's what bringing that minister's going to accomplish. I already don't feel comfortable talking in my own house."

"Okay, Papa."

"What am I supposed to do when a kid gets shot? Let him bleed to death? Tell him, I'm sorry but whitey doesn't want me to help him because he's a danger to democracy and the American way of life?"

"Okay, Papa."

"These kids are doing things. I mean, this free breakfast program is a good thing. They're trying to do things, anyway, and this, this preacher, this Bible-thumper, comes in and—you know that all he's going to finally do is make concessions."

"Okay, Papa."

"Appealing to their Christian souls? Give me a break! Why

isn't the FBI looking for the rednecks who hanged that man out past Hopper? They searched wide and far when those white boys disappeared down in Alabama or wherever the hell it was. Civil rights, my ass. Nonviolence, my ass."

"Let's go in and eat. Come on, Papa."

. . .

COINTELPRO is a code word for "counterintelligence program." By memorandum 2/29/68 the Director authorized submission of 90-day progress letters concerning captioned program for purpose of stimulating thinking in offices where black extremist activities are concentrated. Forty-three offices are currently participating in the project.

. . .

Reskin cleared his throat to announce that he was about to recite grace. He fitted his fist into his palm, set his elbows on each side of his plate, and closed his eyes. He paused to let his silence spread across the table. "Dear Lord," he said, his voice a bit deeper. "First of all, let me ask you a question: Why such a big bird? This is a large tom and I'm not sure I'm worthy of him. But I thank you. We thank you. And thank you for allowing us once again to sit at this table as a family. Please watch over us, protect us, though we may screw our brains out in the room next to our parents." Karen sighed loudly, but Reskin didn't miss a beat. "And watch over our guest. He is a good man. One might hope better for him than my daughter, but you do work in mysterious ways."

"James," Edith complained.

"So, Lord, let us finally say thank you for the lovely meal before us and our health and this fine home, the walls of which continue to reverberate with moans and gasps."

"James!"

"In Jesus' name, amen."

Although upset by her father's so-called prayer, Karen did not cry, but instead loaded up on mashed potatoes and refused turkey.

The turkey was a bit greasy, as game meat is likely to be, and strong in flavor. I couldn't recall a tastier bird.

"So, Robert," Reskin said. "Tell me about your family."

"There's not much to tell. My mother died six years ago. My father, three."

"I'm sorry to hear that," Edith said.

"They're in a better place, you know," said Reskin. "It would have to be. Karen tells me your father was a physician."

"Yes, he was. A GP."

Reskin nodded. "Why didn't you go into medicine?"

"Daddy," Karen whined.

"I guess I just like being outside."

Reskin looked off toward the far wall as if hearing distant music. "I can understand that," he said. "I love being outside too. Maybe I should have gone into hydrology." He laughed. "Do you like your work?"

"Most of the time. Sometimes it's a little tedious." I took a bite of turkey and chewed it while I watched Karen watching me.

"Very tangy," Edith said.

Reskin sat back in his chair and looked at his wife. "If you don't like it, just leave it on your plate."

"I didn't say I didn't like it," Edith said and sighed. "I said it was tangy."

"Of course it's tangy." Reskin stuck a forkload of meat into his mouth and bit down slowly. "Game birds have more flavor than your everyday, force-fed, overweight, crippled, domestic clones." He looked at me. "How do you like it, Robert?"

"It's very good," I said.

"See," he said to Edith. "Robert likes it."

"Jesus Christ," Karen muttered.

Reskin slammed his fork down on the table and rubbed a hand over his face.

"Lighten up," said Edith.

He turned to me again. "Do you hear them? On the one hand, my daughter. A photographer with no visible inroads to the land of talent, an irresponsible sperm bank who excused an act of murder with the words, 'It's my body.'"

"James!" shouted Edith. "That's enough."

Karen was crying, crying so hard that it sounded almost like laughter. She took yet more potatoes, slapping spoonfuls down onto her plate.

"And my wife," Reskin went on. "A political groupie who has intimate fantasies about invalid presidents past."

Karen launched herself from the table; her chair fell to the floor, and she hit the stairs running.

Edith collected herself, breathed deeply, grew larger, stood up, and said, "At least I'm still a Jew." And with that, she too was gone.

. . .

I slept very late, awakened at last by the freezing condition caused by the breakdown of my apartment building's furnace. I tried to call the superintendent, but his line was engaged—which meant that either someone else was complaining or his phone was off the hook, indicating in any event that he was aware of the problem and that at some glacial pace it would be remedied. But what it also meant was that after my shower I would be unable to linger comfortably around my apartment until the afternoon when I hoped that Louise Yellow Calf would meet me at the zoo.

I wandered around Larimer Square for a while, eating more than usual because I was a little anxious—too nervous to sit in one place for long, but apparently not nervous enough to lose my appetite. In fact, I seemed to need food in my hand and mouth constantly. The sun had come out and in Denver's fashion the day was beautiful, promising only forty degrees but looking like seventy. I browsed in a bookstore, then went to the zoo.

In the zoo parking lot, I remembered just how big a place it was, with its various houses of birds and reptiles and its paths leading here and there, to the pachyderms, to the big cats, to the bears. I went to the bears and sat there for a long time watching the polar bears splash around in their pool. The clear weather had brought a number of people out, but still it wasn't crowded and if Louise walked by I'd have no trouble spotting her. A fat couple came and stood in my view of the polar bears, so I moved to a bench in front of the black bears. A man and his little girl wandered by and I watched her escaped red balloon float away over the reptile house. The man and girl came back with hot dogs and chips and sat at the other end of the bench.

"They say I'm a bear dreamer," came the small voice from beside me. It was Louise.

I didn't look at her, nor at the man who was with her. "I'm glad you came."

"I'm sorry about all of this," she said in a subdued voice. "I didn't mean to involve you."

"Well, I'm involved. I'm real involved."

"What can I say?"

"Tell me what happened out there."

"I didn't do it," she said.

"Did you see it happen?"

"No."

"Do you know who did it?"

"No."

"What were you doing out there?"

"I was there to meet them, that's true. But I never even got to talk to them."

I looked around, saw the fat couple buying food at the snack bar and a man policing the area with a broom and cart.

"So, what am I supposed to do?" I asked. I glanced quickly over at her, then back toward the bears. "What are you involved in? I think you owe me that much."

Louise sighed.

"Maybe I can help," I said.

.   .   .

Then it was just me and Reskin in front of the turkey, our wine glasses half full, the candles flickering on the table. We ate on in silence, each taking more turkey. Reskin seemed happy to be there. I remained because I was too exhausted or too much a coward to climb the stairs and face Karen. Sitting there, however, I realized how empty my life was, and I felt more strongly than ever my grandfather's presence. I wasn't very concerned with the recent events of dinner. This family had a long, complex history just as any family does, and I was not about to take sides; I didn't have the energy nor the interest to do so.

Reskin stopped chewing and looked at me. "You think I'm a mean bastard?"

"Yes, I do."

"Are you mad at me?"

I shrugged.

He rubbed his eyes and yawned. "I'm sixty-three years old and I don't know what to do with my life. I don't know if I've done anything so far."

A dog barked somewhere.

Reskin chuckled softly. "You're a smart young fellow. And a hydrologist. You know the ground, the planet. Have you figured out this world?"

I shook my head.

"I read the papers and watch the news and I know they're lying to me. I used to get upset about it. But not anymore. Now I simply find it entertaining." He shook his head as if to shake something loose. "You would think that in over thirty years as a physician I would have learned something about the meaning of life, but, in fact, I haven't. That's sad, isn't it?"

I nodded.

"Damned sad. Life is short."

"Yes, it is."

He took up his half-full wineglass, raised it. "To these sad times," he said.

I drank with him.

.   .   .

Factors such as soil type, weather, slope, and vegetation affect the pro-portion of surface and subsurface water that feeds a stream. Perhaps ⅛ of annual run-off of the hydrologic cycle finds its way to the ocean, while ⅞ filters down into the ground and conducting groundwater. All of a gentle rainfall might infiltrate the ground, but whether it does or not depends on the duration of the precipitation and the nature of the soil.

9

I was sent to my mother's house while Dr. King was staying at my father's. My mother tried to explain to me how important the man was and why I should be proud about his staying at my house, but all I could hear were my grandfather's words.

"I don't see why I can't be there too," I said.

"Because there are a lot of sick people who want to hurt Dr. King. Your father thought it would be better if you were here and I agree with him."

I leaned back in the caned chair and stared past the lace curtains out the window into the yard at the garden shed, which was falling down.

My mother pointed out to me, with her head nodding, that Dr. King was a Christian, and I nodded in rhythm while she let that sink into my head.

I said, "I read that George Wallace is a Christian."

My mother stared at me.

"Did your grandfather tell you that?"

I shook my head.

"George Wallace is no Christian. He's a heathen."

"What about Strom Thurmond?" I knew only that he was a racist from one of the Carolinas.

"Your grandfather's going to go straight to Hell, you know that." My mother was rapidly tapping the kitchen table with the fountain pen she always carried.

"Grandfather says it's whitey's religion." I said it that way, knowing that would get to her.

"Don't talk like that!"

"Well, isn't it?"

"Isn't it what?"

"Whitey's religion?" I pointed to the picture of the blond, blue-eyed Jesus she kept on the wall.

"Your grandfather's going to Hell, you know that."

We just sat there in that familiar quiet and uncomfortable soup that was ours; my mother stared at me as if I were the devil on fire while I stared up at that sickening picture of Christ. I realized then that, for whatever reason, I was loyal to my grandfather. I loved my mother completely, but in my mind I could not find a place for her, understanding somehow even then that I couldn't reconcile her beliefs with my own observations concerning the world. The same arguments about religion and subsequent problematic behavior that had caused her to agree to my living with my father would surface again and again. And the more she would condemn my grandfather and my father for their transgressive thinking, the further away I would drift from her.

· · ·

Article 9. The several tribes of Indians, parties to this treaty, acknowledge their dependence upon the Government of the United States, and agree to be friendly with all the citizens thereof, and commit no depredations upon the person or property of said citizens, and to refrain from carrying on any war upon other Indian tribes; and they further agree that they will not communicate with or assist any persons or nation hostile to the United States, and, further, that they will submit to and obey all laws and regulations which the United States may prescribe for their government and conduct.

· · ·

Upon returning home from the holiday with Karen and her parents I understood that I wanted, needed, and would be ending the relationship—but, whether out of weakness, stupidity, or lazi-ness, I didn't. Instead I walked around shaking my head, knowing that she too saw the break coming; her behavior became more erratic, and her jealousy surfaced more frequently. In the face of her malignant insecurity, even I could see clearly that I was doing neither of us a favor by prolonging things. But we continued to go out to dinners and movies and come home to one or the other's apartment and fuck. There was no such thing as safe sex with her. We of course used condoms and staved off chances of disease, but with each penetration, another nail was driven into our coffin. Her whimpering orgasms left me cold, her pseudo-aggressive ini-tiations of foreplay irritated me, and her obsession with her weight sent me plummeting into sleep. We would lie in bed and she would open her mouth, letting out the words *weight* or *fat* and I would be gone, dreaming somewhere in my head about fishing alone on a stream. All the while, I guess because I felt guilty for beginning the relationship, I attempted to convince her that I cared about her. I had proven to myself that all the warnings from friends were justified, but I was too *kind* to hurt her feelings. So, instead I let things hang on and ended up hurting her even more.

· · ·

It was strange standing in the dining room and looking out at the side yard where the dog lived. There had never been a window on that wall and now most of the wall was gone, blackened bricks were strewn about, two-by-fours were shattered and exposed. The furni-ture and the remaining adjacent walls were charred badly and smoke still rose from spots. My grandfather kicked through the rubble while my father stood beside me with his hand on my shoulder.

"Were you here when it happened?" I asked, my eyes riveted to the hole in the house.

"Yes," my father said, clearing his throat. "We were sitting at the table in the kitchen. Whoever it was drove by and threw the bomb against the side of the house."

"Damn crackers," my grandfather said, taking a long deep breath. "And you know, the damn insurance company won't cover it. Wait, you'll see. That lily white agent will come out here and say it was arson and that'll be it. Damn crackers."

"Son," my father said, "I want you to stay with your mother for a while."

I shook my head.

"You'll have to," he said.

My grandfather walked toward us, kicking at a piece of a chair. "Just for a little while."

.   .   .

I never did get a good look at Louise in the little-girl get-up, as I kept my eyes the whole time on my feet, the bears, or the fat people. She asked me at one point how well I knew the mountain and I told her I knew it very well, that I had studied it during all seasons.

"Will you come and talk to some friends of mine tonight?" she asked.

"Talk about what?" I pushed at a cigarette butt on the ground with the toe of my shoe.

"Will you come?"

"I'll come. Where?"

"Good. Be at the Sidewinder Tavern downtown, tonight at nine-thirty."

"Okay. Want to tell me more?"

"Tonight."

.   .   .

This program has as its objectives the neutralization of black extremist groups, the prevention of violence by these groups, and the prevention of a coalition of black extremist organizations. Since these offices have participated significantly in this program, it is felt we can now relax our administrative procedures by eliminating the 90-day letter. We will not suffer from this discontinuance, as continued participation in this program by field is followed by individual Supervisors in Racial Intelligence Section, Domestic Intelligence Division. In addition, the Inspection Division analyzes each office's participation in this program during field-office inspections. In view of the above and to streamline our operations, it is recommended these progress letters be discontinued. No change is required in any Bureau manual.

. . .

The heat was back on when I returned to my apartment, and although it hadn't been on for long, the sun through the window had cooked the air and made it bearable. I unpacked the groceries I'd picked up on the way and put a kettle on for tea. I stood in the kitchen, leaned against the sink, and watched the kettle. I made the tea and sat at the table. I wondered what I was going to find out tonight, wondered whether I needed to worry about being followed, and realized immediately that I didn't know how not to be followed and wouldn't be able to detect anyone tracing my movements anyway. I would just take for granted that Louise understood that.

About halfway through my cup of tea there was a knock at the door. I looked at the clock on the bookcase and saw that it was nearly seven o'clock. I was dreading the prospect of seeing Karen as I walked to the door, but somehow the rapping on the wood didn't sound urgent enough to be hers. I opened the door and there was Gladys Davies, half smiling through what I immediately and clearly recognized as a condition just this side of intoxication.

"Hello, Mr. Hawks," she said. "May I come in?"

I stepped aside and let her enter, realizing as she walked passed me that she was in her stocking feet and carrying her black pumps.

"Didn't you get my messages?" she asked.

"No. My machine's been acting up lately." I wondered why it was so easy for me to lie to her.

She sat down on the sofa and leaned back, blew out a long breath. "It's just a little chilly in here, isn't it?"

"The heat was off in the building for a while," I said. "What do you want?"

She looked at me with that shine covering her eyes and a slow smile found her face. "I'm from the FBI. Remember? I know you remember. You're in way over your head Mr. Hawks." She rubbed a hand over her face. "Listen, do you have any coffee?"

"I have tea." I was still standing by the door. "Do you have a warrant or something?"

"Nope. I don't need one. Your little friend is a very bad person who hangs out with very bad people. Did you know that? She would just as soon cut your throat as look at you."

"I don't know who you're talking about."

"The woman who runs the store up near your cabin seems to recall seeing her get out of your truck."

"Clara's damn near blind," I said. Then, "I might have given a young woman a ride and then I might not have. You're telling me that the woman at the store only *seems* to recall the incident. Are you always drunk?"

"No," she said curtly. "You don't have coffee?"

"Only tea."

"That's right, the tea drinker." She looked out the window, then back at me. "Her name is Louise Yellow Calf, aka Louise Small Calf, aka Lois Yeager. You got any akas?"

I walked across the room to the chair in front of the sofa and sat on the arm. "What would your superiors say if I called them and told them you were drunk in my apartment?"

Davies reached into her pocketbook and pulled out a card. "Here," she said, leaning forward and handing it to me. "The office number is on there. Just call and let's see what they say."

I held it in my fingers and studied it. Then there was another knock at the door, a rapid, uneven knock and I thought "Why not?" as I walked to the door and opened it.

It was indeed Karen and she was standing there with a large bouquet of brightly colored flowers. She said, "I'm sorry, I'm sorry, I'm sorry." Three times, just like that, quickly. Then she saw Davies and opened her mouth as wide as any human being I had ever seen and let go with a scream that rattled the whole building.

I stepped back from the noise and ended up standing beside Davies, who had gained her feet.

"I was right all along!" Karen shouted.

"There's nothing going on here," Davies said, surprising me. I glanced over at her and saw that she was a bit unsteady on her feet. She sat back down.

Karen kicked the flowers and slammed the door and I was horrified to see that she was on the same side of it as I was. "I need to talk to someone," she said, stepping past me and sitting on the chair opposite the sofa.

"There's really nothing going on," Davies said. I recognized in Davies face the same look she had shown just before passing out in the restaurant.

"Why are you here?" Karen asked, shaking her head, her voice beginning to crack.

"I'm just here talking to Mr. Hawks."

"Are you going to take a shower this time?"

I grabbed my coat and stepped to the door. From there I looked back at them—one drunk, one crazy—and they were talking to each other. I left the apartment, kicking the rest of the flowers inside before I closed the door.

An old man who was a neighbor said to me as I walked by, "Can't you keep that girlfriend of yours quiet?"

"I'm really trying. She's in that apartment talking to the FBI right now. I hope that does the trick."

"Well, good," he said and slammed his door.

.   .   .

Except as otherwise expressly provided by enactment of Congress, any offense against the United States begun in one district and completed in another may be inquired of and prosecuted in any district in which the offense was begun or completed.

The molecular layer is thick in the hippocampus and contains a large number of Golgi bodies.

I understood the story to have been this: Tad Johnson was an out-spoken leader of the Black Panther Party in our city. He had been arrested a couple of times and shot once, but since the shooting he had a bodyguard and kept a high profile, although he moved from apartment to apartment frequently. He went to California and met with the BPP leadership out there and was told he would become the new spokesperson for the Party. Another man, a black man—although my grandfather referred to him as a cracker—a man named Reynolds Stoddard, who was a security officer for the Party, met with an FBI agent when he and Johnson returned from California and told the FBI of the upcoming advancement. Despite Johnson's arrests and his having been wounded, the FBI saw Richmond's chapter of the BPP gaining momentum. So, in the Red Steak restaurant, Stoddard sat with two FBI agents and drew a detailed floor plan of the apartment in which Johnson was staying, showing the placement of furniture, closets, and windows. He also made a list of the weapons that were kept by Johnson and the bodyguard who would also be sleeping in the apartment. Johnson taught a political awareness course at a local Holy Roller church, then went home with several Party members. Stoddard was with them, but left at 12:30 A.M. Ronald Taylor, who was asleep in the front room with a shotgun across his lap, barely had time to stand when the front door was kicked in and a round from a .30 caliber M-1 carbine tore open his chest. He died in-stantly as his finger squeezed off one round. The cop, one of eight, shot Brendell Lewis, who was then struck by a bullet from the pistol of another officer. Another cop stepped in with his .45 caliber Thompson submachine gun and fired through the walls into the bedroom; one bullet struck a sleeping Johnson in the thigh. Into the bedroom the raiders marched and each servant of the people fired one round into Johnson's head.

I listened to the story as it was told to my grandfather and father several times. I was sitting on the stairs when I was supposed to be asleep. One Panther who had been there survived and was arrested for possession of marijuana. Some months later, I heard that the charges were dropped. I was fourteen and just beginning to catch the attention of white policemen when I walked down the street. It scared me. I found that I was angry because I had to be scared. I was angry because I had to worry about how I was walking or where I was walking, whether it looked as if I were running, or whether I had too much money or too little money in my pocket, or whether something had happened two blocks over involving a "nigger who looked just like me." The flashing lights of a police car made me and my friends hold our breath.

. . .

A partially ordered set A *is said to be well ordered if and only if every nonempty subset* X *of* A *has a greatest lower bound in* X.

. . .

I found the Sidewinder Tavern easily. I was about half an hour early and I sat in a booth near the back, partly in the shadows, but I wanted Louise to be able to spot me, so I sat on the outer edge of the seat. I ordered a beer and waited while listening to a loud and rather bad blues band that featured a woman lead singer with a lisp. As I raised my mug to my lips I found that my hand was shaking. I had been bothered more than I realized by Davies's sudden visit and the subsequent reunion of the agent and Karen. I wondered if they were still in my apartment, if Davies had passed out, as was her wont, which would give Karen the opportunity to take the agent's pistol from her bag, shoot her, and leave the blame with me. A couple of rowdy fellows got into a shoving match not too far from me and one of them stumbled into my table. I pushed him back into the fray and observed that he had left on my table a note. I read it discreetly. "Go to the bathroom," it said. I looked around the bar and then stood up, took another pull on my beer and walked to the back of the joint and into the men's room. A blond man passed me on his way out. There were two Indian men standing inside by the sinks. One was tallish with long hair and the other was about my size, darker, with short hair, wearing a plaid shirt, a denim jacket, and a faded Yankees baseball cap.

"Take off your jacket and shirt," the taller of the two men said. I noticed that the other man had shed his jacket and was unbuttoning his shirt.

I did as I was told. We exchanged clothes and the shorter man left the rest room. The taller man put the cap on my head, pulling the brim down tightly, and nodded.

"What now?" I asked.

"Just follow me."

I did. He led the way back through the tavern and we passed the man who was now wearing my shirt and field jacket, huddled into the corner of the booth I had been occupying. Outside, we got into a yellow 1972 Monte Carlo and drove circuitously through downtown, only to abandon the car just blocks from the tavern and duck into the back of a Chevy van. The van was driven by a large woman who didn't look back at me.

"My name is Dexter," the tall man said finally and shook my hand. "That's Carlotta driving." He pointed, then snapped a cigarette free from his pack and offered me one.

"No, thanks."

"It's not far," he said.

· · ·

I was born a Lakota and I have lived a Lakota and I shall die a Lakota.
Taku Skanskan is familiar with my spirit and when I die I will go with
him. Then I will be with my forefathers. If this is not the heaven of the
white man, I shall be satisfied.

· · ·

The policeman standing in our living room was a black man. He
was stout, although not tall, and wore tortoiseshell glasses that,
from my view, seemed cartoonishly thick. He never sat down, just
asked my father not where my grandfather had gone, but when he
was expected back. My father told the officer that he would be
back shortly and that he was welcome to wait, to have a seat if
he liked, but he remained standing. I sat near him, on the sofa,
leaning forward, my elbows on my knees, and watched the way he
swayed back and forth on the balls of his feet. I was fourteen and
I was finding every day that I was angrier and angrier, and watching him now was like a wooden splinter digging its way under my
fingernail.

"You don't mind if I carry on with what I was doing?" my
father asked politely, then excused himself from the living room
and went back to his desk in the study.

To the policeman, I said, "Do you have a gun?"

He just looked at me, no expression on his face.

"Do they give guns to black people in the police department?"
I asked, trying to see under his plaid jacket.

He didn't like what I was saying and so probably took a dislike
to me, but he didn't say anything, just rocked there on the balls of

his flat feet. I studied his eyes behind his lenses, which seemed to be fixed on the empty fireplace.

"Would you shoot a black person?" I asked.

The cop sighed and then looked at me. "If I thought he was going to shoot me, yes," he responded.

I nodded, feeling somehow safe, perhaps because I was in my own home. "Have you ever shot anybody?"

"No. And I hope I don't have to."

"What do you want with my grandfather?"

"I'm just here to ask him a few questions."

"Are you going to arrest him?"

"Should I?"

It hit me then that this cop wasn't as stupid as I had assumed. I studied his soft-soled black shoes and white socks, one of which had a small hole at the ankle. I was about to ask him why he'd become a policeman when my grandfather came into the house through the front door. He stopped when he saw the man, then pushed the door gently closed. "May I help you?" my grandfather asked.

"I'm Detective Leroy Hanes," the man said and he shook my grandfather's hand. "Are you Dr. Henry Hawks?"

"Yes, I am."

"Then we agree that I have talked to you?"

My grandfather nodded.

"Then I can be on my way. Thank you for your time." With that, the policeman stepped politely past my grandfather and left through the front door.

. . .

Carlotta drove the van carefully, not quite slowly. I could see through the cracked windshield, so I had an idea where we were headed. We passed through an industrial section of town with warehouses and semi-trailers lining the street, into a neighborhood that I, like most people who didn't live there, attempted to avoid. It was an area of town known for its poverty and, more importantly and impressively, its gang violence. The night had become cold and I realized that the jacket that I had received in trade back at the tavern was not as warm as my own. I buttoned it up and folded my arms and then we were there. At least, Carlotta had stopped the van.

We got out and I saw that we were in front of a shell of a one-story house: a porch with no rail ran the width of its front, and all the windows showed light inside. It wasn't until I was on the porch and at the solid, white door that I saw that a man with a shotgun across his lap was sitting in a chair in the shadows. I was startled and although I could see his face clearly, he didn't turn to look at me at all.

The inside was well lighted but not bright. The front door opened into the living room, which was furnished with patio chairs, the metal kind with bent tubing for legs, and a heavy, exceptionally ugly, lopsided green sofa with three men sitting shoulder to shoulder, facing a game show on television. I stood near the door and peered into the next room, which was the kitchen. I could see the sink and a corner of the stove, and I could hear the rattle of the refrigerator motor. A man about my size came out of the kitchen and approached me. His eyes were deeply set, and he wore his hair pulled back and tied behind his head in what I would later see was a braid. He shook my hand and told me his name was Tyrone Bisset. He welcomed me, saying, "We are the American Indian Revolution."

I recognized his name. He had been tried for the murders of yet two other FBI men on the Cold Deer Reservation in South Dakota. He hadn't been convicted, I remembered that—much of the evidence of the government turned out to be fabricated or altered—but I believed also that he was still a fugitive. Bisset introduced the other men in the room. On the sofa were John and Leonard Hat, twins, and Matthew Crow Feather, who all nodded to me in turn. Carlotta's last name was Looking Horse and Dexter's was Peacock.

"Louise tells me you know the Plata Mountain area very well," Bisset said, pointing to an empty chair.

I sat and felt the chair give. "I know it fairly well," I said.

"You've studied the mountain?"

"I'm a hydrologist and I've studied the Plata watershed pretty extensively." I looked at Bisset's eyes, trying to draw a bead on what he wanted from me.

Something happened on the game show that caused Matthew Crow Feather to laugh out loud. I looked over at him and saw the traces of his smile fade again into expressionlessness. No one showed a reaction, not even an acknowledgment of his having laughed. Then, as if he were reliving the moment, Matthew Crow Feather laughed again. When I looked at him this time he continued to laugh. The twins turned to watch him and Bisset did as well. Carlotta and Dexter had gone into the kitchen.

His laughter held in, Crow Feather talked. "I saw this old man on television and he was a medicine man and the white man asked what kind of feathers he used and he said, 'Eagle feathers and hawk feathers and even Woody Woodpecker feathers.'" Matthew exploded once again and the others laughed with him. "I only just remembered that," he said. The laughter died down and again the three men on the sofa attended to the television.

"Do you think you could find your way from the lake over the mountain and through the forest to the northern edge of the Plata Reservation?" Bisset asked me.

I answered quickly. "Sure. Dog Creek to Silly Man Canyon would be one way. Why?"

"Is it a difficult hike? I mean, how far is it?"

"I don't know." I looked at the ceiling and thought about it. "I'd say it's about twenty miles. It's pretty rugged country, depending on the time of year. Why?"

"Are you hungry? I'm hungry."

. . .

Although it hurts me deeply, I am forced to the conclusion that the prosecution in this trial had something other than attaining justice foremost in its mind. The fact that incidents of misconduct formed a pattern throughout the course of the trial leads me to the belief that this case was not prosecuted in good faith or in the spirit of justice. The waters of justice have been polluted, and dismissal, I believe, is the appropriate cure for the pollution in this case.

. . .

I owned a royal blue 1955 Studebaker pickup with a wraparound rear window. It ran most of the time, and the colder it got, the more reliable the truck seemed to be. There was another truck just like it in Denver. I would see it parked in various lots downtown quite regularly, although I never saw the owner, I envied the person— that truck had better tires than mine.

I had just broken up with Karen for the second time. It wasn't clear to me that we had ever actually gotten back together and I was certainly unclear about how the reunion had come about. Getting "back together" had consisted of one dinner and my telling her that I was sure things wouldn't work out. The day following the dinner I returned to my office from lunch to discover some twenty messages from Karen. I put the stack of yellow sheets with my things and took them with me up to Plata Mountain, where I had work to do. At the junction, I glanced into my case, saw the messages, felt sorry for Karen, and went into the store to use the phone. Karen answered the phone anxiously, as was her wont, and immediately asked me where I was calling from.

"I'm up on the mountain. Are you okay?"

"Up on the mountain? How did you get there?"

"I drove." I told her.

"Drove what?"

"My truck. Listen, I'm sorry I called . . ."

But the phone was dropped and I could hear loud, uncontrolled sobbing in the background. Karen's roommate Heidi picked up the phone and she asked me where I was calling from.

"Plata Mountain," I said, blankly. "I drove my truck up this afternoon. What's going on?"

"Karen stole *your* truck," Heidi said.

I leaned away from the phone and peered out the window at my Studebaker. "I don't think so, Heidi."

"Karen and the guy across the street just parked your truck in front of our house," Heidi said.

"I see." It was not difficult to figure out what had happened. "It's not my business." I hung up.

11

Title 18, United States Code, Section 2383, Section 2384, Section 2385

. . .

My father was dropping me off at my mother's so that he and my grandfather could fly to Atlanta where my grandfather would testify for a man named Bunchy Cooke. I didn't know it at the time, but I found out later that Bunchy Cooke was the man from whom my grandfather had extracted a bullet while I watched in that little house off Reynolds Road. Bunchy Cooke had been accused of killing a white couple on a tennis court in a park in downtown Atlanta: three people swore that they had seen him and another man commit the crime. But, as it happened, the murders were carried out on the very day and at the same time that my grandfather was treating Bunchy Cooke's gunshot wound.

"Do you think he should go down there and testify?" my mother asked my father. She put her arm around me and held me close. I was a good head taller than she was by that time.

My father just shook his head, not as a response, but a reaction to her question.

I pulled gently away from my mother, sat on the sofa, and watched my father's face. I realized that, for my father, having my grandfather was like having another son, a wild son with whom you couldn't argue, nor, in reasonable fashion, disagree, except to remind him of the danger involved in his movements and actions.

"He wants to do it," my father said. "I don't know what else he can do."

I understood from the talk around my house and the reports of the police visits and questions that my grandfather's furtive treatment of Bunchy Cooke's gunshot wound was illegal. I became afraid as I realized that Grandfather, in supplying Bunchy Cooke's alibi, would be incriminating himself.

"I want to go," I said, standing.

"No." My mother responded quickly.

"I want to go."

"It's better that you stay here, Rob," my father said.

"I'm a teenager," I said. "I understand what's going on. I want to go." I felt older at that moment, the anger in me felt directed. "I want to be with Grandfather."

I think my father wanted to say yes, but when he looked at my mother and saw the way her hands were shaking, he said, "I want you stay here, Rob."

. . .

I sat between the twins at the table in the kitchen and we ate hamburgers that arrived with another man named Charlie Runs Far. John Hat was talkative and he pointed at me with french fries as he made points. "If you're an Indian, you don't believe in civil rights. It simply doesn't make sense. They come and talk about equality again and again, but they always lie. Right, Leonard?"

Leonard Hat nodded.

"Besides," John Hat continued, "we're not American citizens. We're Indians. We're American Americans. You know, when we get this continent back, all you black people will have to leave."

They all laughed and I found myself laughing softly with them.

"Where is Louise?" I asked.

"She'll be here a little later," Bisset said. He was sitting directly opposite me and was now lighting a cigarette with a wooden match. He shook the match out and it dropped on the paper in which his burger had been wrapped. "She says you helped her out in a big way."

"Not really," I said. "I just kept her from freezing to death out in the snow. That's all."

Matthew Crow Feather looked at me and laughed, nodding his head as if with approval.

"Do you know anything about the FBI agents who were killed up at Plata Mountain?" I asked.

"You cut right to it, don't you?" Bisset said. He exhaled a cloud of blue smoke and scratched his chin with the same hand that held his cigarette. "What would you say if I told you the agents who were up there wanted to help us, wanted to give us some information that could help us out?"

I shrugged. "I don't know what I'd say. Is that in fact what you're saying?"

"Louise didn't shoot them," Bisset said.

I pushed my half-eaten burger away and looked at the stack of dishes in the sink. "What's it like to be a fugitive?" I asked.

He looked at me, then said, "Actually, I'm not wanted for anything."

"Officially," Leonard Hat added.

"Officially," Bisset said, leaning back in his chair.

"Sorry," I said.

"Why? For all I know, by now I *am* wanted for something." His easy smiled faded, he leaned forward, and he asked me if I'd ever heard of an anthrax bomb.

"An anthrax bomb?" I asked. "You mean, like the disease cattle catch?"

Bisset nodded. "I'll tell you a little story. In 1942, the British started trying to make a bomb that would eliminate livestock, soldiers, everybody. They used anthrax. They set one off on an island in Gruinard Bay over there in Scotland. The island is still contaminated. Nobody can go there. All the rabbits turned black. The United States government bought the bombs or took them or whatever. The army has been illegally storing anthrax bombs and other kinds of biochemical agents on the north end of the reservation."

I didn't believe what he was telling me, but I didn't know why I didn't believe him. The government was doing secret experiments, like the Tuskegee thing, all the time, and I realized that that was the scariest part of all, that in spite of knowledge of past transgressions, I still resisted belief in a new one, somehow believing that my country was somehow me, maybe. But it wasn't my country.

"In underground tanks."

Matthew Crow Feather groaned.

"How do you know?" I asked.

"We know."

I looked at his eyes and I saw that he, at least, believed his story. I shook my head slowly. "If what you're saying is true . . ." I stopped and pictured the terrain in my head. "It depends on where the stuff is. Any leaks would be carried by the groundwater to Silly Man Creek right into the Plata or down the Dog into the lake or simply into the aquifer. It's all wells on the reservation."

Tyrone Bisset was nodding.

. . .

Each and every cranial nerve is attached to some part of the surface of the brain, but these fibers also extend deep into the nucleus of the brain, the center of the gray matter. The nerves emerge from the brain, pass through tubular prolongations in the dura mater and leave the skull through foramina at its base, on the way to their final destination.

. . .

James Reskin was the last person I expected to greet at the door of my place in Denver. It was about seven in the evening, a week or so after the new year, and I had been going over some aerial photographs spread out on the coffee table. He stepped into my apartment with a nervous, brisk stride, pacing back to the door once he was fully in, then bouncing over to the sofa and sitting with his legs apart, his elbows on his knees, his face in his gloved hands.

I stood at the door, which was still open, the knob of it still in my hand, staring at him, wondering how best to put "What the hell are you doing here?" but he spoke first.

"I heard you broke up with my little girl," is what he said, lifting his face and looking at me.

I closed the door, but still stood by it.

He went on, "She called all upset, saying that you were a monster who couldn't love anybody but yourself, but you've probably already heard all that. Anyway, good for you. You're too good for her. She'll drag you down into the pit and sewer with her and you'll never climb out. So, I say, good for you." He took a long, deliberate breath. "But that's not why I'm here."

I walked over to the chair beside him and sat on the edge of it. "It's not?"

"No, Robert, I just want to talk."

"Talk."

"You know that I am an unhappy man." There was no need for his waiting for a signal of agreement from me. "Isaiah 38:1 says, 'Set thine house in order: for thou shalt die, and not live.' Well, Robert, you've seen my house."

I nodded.

"'Thou shalt die and not live.' How about that? What do you think?" He leaned forward and started to push around the photographs on the coffee table.

"I don't know what to say," I said. "What do you want to talk about?" His eyes were on the photos. I noticed his down-filled parka and I realized that I was warm without a sweater. "Would you like to take off your coat?"

"No, thank you. I'm still a little cold, in fact." He looked at me with weak eyes.

"Did you just drive all the way from Santa Fe?"

"Yes."

"I'll make you some tea, okay? That'll warm you up." I walked over to the kitchen area and began to fill the kettle from the tap.

"You've seen my house, haven't you?" he asked. "By house, you know I mean my family, my life."

"I've seen it," I said.

I switched on the burner with its familiar clicking until there was a flame and placed the kettle over it, then turned to see that Reskin was holding a pistol. He held it in his lap, rubbing his hands over it as if it were a smooth ball. Hesitantly, I walked back to Reskin and sat on the chair beside the sofa.

"This is a .32 caliber pistol," he said. "It's not a big gun. Do you think it will do the job?"

"What job would that be?"

"If I put the barrel in my mouth and pull the trigger, will this pistol kill me for sure?"

"You're the doctor," I said and I was wondering if I could get to the telephone without tipping him any further.

"Yeah, I'm the doctor. 'Physician, heal thyself.' Is that how that saying goes?"

"You're full of sayings tonight," I said and smiled stupidly at him. "Did you say it's a .32? I've shot a .38 before, but never a .32. Would you mind if I took a look at it?"

"I don't think so."

"Does your wife know where you are?"

"What the hell does she care? The heathen." He pinched the bridge of his nose and closed his eyes for a second, then looked at me. "You believe in Jesus, don't you?"

My instinct was to lie, but instead, I said, "No, I don't."

"So you're a heathen as well," he said.

"I'm afraid so."

His eyes fell to the weapon in his lap. He shook his head. "Yea, though I walk through the valley of death, I shall fear no evil. His staff, blah, blah, blah."

"You don't really want to shoot yourself."

"Yes, I pretty much do," he said, calmly.

"To answer your earlier question—No, I don't think a little pistol like that is a sure killer. You'll more than likely fire the bullet just far enough into your brain to become a vegetable."

"You think so?"

I nodded. "May I look at it more closely?" I asked.

He held it toward me for a closer look, but he didn't intend to give it to me. As luck would have it, the whistle of the kettle startled him and he dropped the thing. I picked it up and stepped away toward the boiling water.

"Give it back," he said, standing.

"Wait a second," I said. I was over the sink now and unloading the pistol. "Let me get the tea and then we can talk and then I'll give it back to you."

"You promise?"

"I'm getting the tea."

Reskin sat back down.

.   .   .

Those were anxious days, when my grandfather was in Atlanta testifying for Bunchy Cooke. Even my mother was worried about him. She was trying to keep busy by making me cookies and soup and asking me what were my favorite foods now that I was a teen-ager. An hour didn't go by that I failed to think of Grandfather. I imagined him standing up like in the movies and the clerk asking him to put his hand on the Bible and swear, and him declining the opportunity by saying, "As much as I'd love to press my hand upon that book to ensure it stays shut, I will pass and take a civil oath."

My mother had just set a plate of cookies on the coffee table and settled down with a book when she looked at me and said, "You're concerned about your grandfather, aren't you?"

I nodded. "What would you do?" I asked. "If somebody came here with a wound, would you help him?"

"Yes, I would."

"Would you call the police?"

My mother studied my face and I knew she was trying to find an answer that was instructive, that would serve me later in life, so that if anything bad ever happened to me she could, at least, dis-solve some guilt by the thought that she had tried to teach me better.

"Would you call the police?" I asked again.

Still she had no answer as she played with the corner of a page of the book in her lap.

"Neither would I," I said.

Bisset looked at me from across the table and asked flat out, "How much money do you have?"

"On me?"

"No, all together, everything."

"I've got some savings. A few thousand, I guess. Why?"

"May we have it?"

"No."

And that was that. There didn't seem to be any hard feelings or any second thinking about my response. My "no" was simply accepted. "How do you guys support yourselves on the run like this? If this is being on the run."

"We used to get checks for our land," John Hat said. "Good old Form 5-5525. How much land do we own, Leonard?"

"One-ninety," Leonard said. He was drinking a beer now and peeling the label from the bottle.

"Yeah, the BIA used to collect the lease money from the white rancher who grazes his cattle there and send us a check four times a year. But now, since we've been in AIR, the checks don't come. The rancher still grazes his cattle, but the checks don't come. We still have the same post office box in Mobridge, but the checks don't come."

Bisset coughed and got up to fill a glass with water from the tap. "We get money by asking the way I just asked you. Sometimes, people just give us money. Sometimes. We work, but that's hard because the FBIs come to the job and ask around, and then no more job."

Louise entered through the back door with the man she had been with at the zoo. She smiled politely at me, but not in a way that suggested friendship. "You've met everyone?"

"Yes," I said.

"This is Dicky Kills Enemy," Louise introduced the man with her, not pausing as she moved to set down the small paper sack she was carrying on the counter.

I stood and shook his hand. Looking at his face, I recognized something in it. "Are you Hiram's son?"

"Grandson."

I could see the resemblance not so much to Hiram but to the uniformed man in the photograph on Hiram's wall, the son killed *by* the Korean War.

"We didn't shoot any FBIs," Bisset said to me, turning us all back to why I had been chasing Louise.

"I believe you," I said.

The phone rang and Leonard Hat picked up and listened. He put the receiver down. "Cops on the way."

My head was swimming now as I found myself being hurried out and into a midseventies Ford sedan with Louise, Bisset, and the twins. Matthew, Carlotta, and the others piled into the van and we left the house with the lights on inside. I understood what was going on and I also comprehended the gravity of their situation, if not their complete story. It was painfully familiar to me, and for whatever reasons—sincere or stupidly romantic—I was sympathetic to these people. Bisset drove the Ford, its lifters knocking under the hood, and Louise sat in the back between me and John Hat. The car smelled of motor oil, gasoline, and fried food.

"Biochemical agents?" I said, the sound of it unreal in my head and mouth.

Louise looked at me. "We're not sure. That's what those FBIs were going to tell us. They said they had documentation."

"So what were they, Indian sympathizers or something?" I adjusted my feet on the floor, which was cluttered with cans and loose papers. "I mean, how did they know about it?"

"We don't know how they knew," Bisset said. "The FBI men have been hanging around some of the rez's forever, especially since we started mentioning stuff that wasn't right. They help out the "apples" on the reservations. One of the FBIs who got killed was an Indian, the other one was black. They were supposedly trying to help us. That's what they said they were doing. The Indian was from Florida, a Seminole."

Hearing that made me think of Davies and how odd it was that she alone was investigating the case, especially given her predilection for alcohol. It all felt wrong, the FBI story, the story I was getting now. A light snow began to fall. I noticed the flakes as we waited for the stoplight at a busy intersection. People crossed the street in front of us; some tried to see through the windshield.

"Where are we heading?" I asked.

"We're going to let you out pretty soon," Bisset said, rolling down his window a little so he could flick the glowing ashes of his cigarette outside.

I turned to Louise. "Just tell me half of what you know. I'll settle for that," I said. I wanted to learn something before I was asked to get out of the car.

"You know all there is to know," Bisset said, glancing at me through the rearview mirror. "But you can tell me something. Why did you lie to the FBI?"

"I don't like the FBI," I said quickly.

"Just like that," Bisset said.

"Just like that."

"Man doesn't like the FBI," John Hat said.

"You want to hear a funny thing?" Bisset said. "We don't know that mountain very well. I mean, like, Dicky Kills Enemy, that's his reservation, but he doesn't even know the mountain. He's essentially a city boy."

"What are you saying?"

"He grew up mostly in Los Angeles. He doesn't know the land, like where the canyons go and how to get from one place to another quickly without being seen and all that."

"And that's where I come in," I said. "That's why you came to the zoo." I was looking down at Louise, but she didn't look back.

"You don't have money," Bisset said.

.   .   .

I pushed Reskin's unloaded pistol down into the front pocket of my trousers, which was very uncomfortable, and then took the tea over to him. I blew on mine and took a sip, but he just put his mug down on top of the photographs and leaned back into the sofa. He pinched the bridge of his nose again and seemed to sway a bit.

"Would you like me to call Karen?" I asked. "If you give me the number I can call your wife."

"No."

"I think I ought to call someone."

He waved a hand at me as if he didn't care what I did, then, becoming aware of his gloves, peeled them off and shook his hands as if they were going to sleep on him.

I got up and moved toward the phone, but stopped as I noticed the man's eyes. They were bloodshot and weak, but why not?—he had just driven all the way from Santa Fe. Still, I knew there was something else—his pupils seemed dilated. I could feel my heart beginning to race.

"Dr. Reskin, did you do something?"

"What do you mean?"

"Did you take something?"

He looked at me and I could see that he was all screwed up inside, that he couldn't focus, that he was lost and scared, and his body was covered with the trembling I had so many times observed on his daughter.

"Aw, shit," I said and in spite of his weak protest, I picked up the phone and dialed 911 and told the dispatcher that I thought my friend had just taken an overdose of some kind of medicine.

Reskin tried to stand, then fell across the sofa, muttering to himself. "Look at my house," he said. "Look at my house. There is no order. Look at my house."

I called Karen.

"Oh, Robert, Robert, I'm so glad it's you. I'm sorry about everything," Karen said.

"That's not why I'm calling. It's about your father."

"Oh, him," she said with disdain. "Well, what about him?"

"He's here in my apartment."

"He's what?"

"He drove up from New Mexico and there's something wrong with him. The ambulance is on the way."

"He's at your apartment?"

"Listen to me, Karen. I think he's tried to kill himself. He told me he wants to die. I think he took something. He's all weird. I'm going to ask the paramedics to take him to Mercy. That's the closest hospital. Mercy. Did you get that?"

"Okay, okay."

. . .

President Truman: *The bill makes perfectly clear what many men and women, here and abroad, have failed to recognize, that in our transactions with the Indian tribes we have at least since the Northwest Ordinance of 1787 set for ourselves the standard of fair and honorable dealings, pledging respect for all Indian property rights. . . . It would be*

a miracle if in the course of these dealings—the largest real estate trans-
action in history—we had not made some mistakes. . . . We stand ready
to correct any mistakes we have made.

. . .

The story of my grandfather's presence in Atlanta and willing-
ness to testify was reported several times in our city newspaper,
along with a photo that didn't look much like him and some scary
editorials and letters to the editor. My grandfather was called a
troublemaker, a black militant, a criminal, and—by someone who
allegedly signed her letter "A Black Woman From Hopper"—he
was called a "no-good-who-was-old-enough-to-know-better."
My father called two days after they left for Atlanta and told me,
after my insistent inquiry, that the prosecution was trying to keep
my grandfather from taking the witness stand.

"Is Grandfather okay?" I asked.

"He's fine, son. Don't worry."

"There's all sorts of stuff in the paper here."

"Well, don't let it bother you. I'll talk to you later, Rob. Put
your mother on."

I handed the phone to my mother and I watched as she listened, watched as her face registered more and more concern,
watched until she finally hung up.

"What is it?" I asked.

"Rob," she said, in her serious voice. "I want to you to stay
close to the house for the next few days."

"Why?"

"Just promise me you will."

"What's going on? What's wrong? What did Dad say?"

My mother got mad, the vein in her neck pushing out and
making her look like a bird and she shouted, "Just stay close! Do
you have to be that way—just like him? Them! Just stay close!"

. . .

We were near Aurora on a pretty busy highway when Bisset pulled the Ford off to the side and waited quietly. I understood this as my cue to get out so I did, and then I watched the car's lights disappear into the sea of other taillights headed west. I looked at my watch and saw that it was near two. I walked away from the highway and followed the exit ramp toward a gas station that turned out to be closed. The temperature had dropped another several degrees and the snow was falling now in earnest. I then spotted the sign of a Denny's restaurant some blocks away and started walking toward it. Trucks sped by me, spraying me with the road's spittle, and I was more than a little nervous so I moved farther onto the shoulder and walked through the slush and roadside debris. When the headlights of the oncoming cars and trucks forced my eyes down I saw that my boots were soaked and caked with mud.

The Denny's was at least warm. A short chat with the short waitress yielded the information that I was some eight or nine miles from downtown Denver and so about that far from my apartment. I sat at the counter, nursed a cup of tea, and choked down a wedge of apple pie, which looked just like its menu mugshot, while I tried to figure out a way home. I laughed to myself, thinking that I had been stranded in all sorts of places, snowed in on mountains, broken down in the desert, but here I was in a city, just miles from my house and I couldn't get home. I knew I could walk, but it was cold and wet and to tell the truth, I was scared out there with all those crazies. Bears and rattlesnakes are never as frightening as people. Besides, I could feel how cold my toes had gotten already in my wet boots as the heat of the restaurant brought the painful feeling back into them.

The short waitress came back. I looked at her impossibly blue eyes and her poorly painted lips. A fat man mopped the floor in the nonsmoking section of the dining area.

"I guess you don't get many customers at this hour," I said, trying to relax myself with small talk.

"Not normal-looking fellas like you," she said.

.   .   .

I had been walking for nearly an hour and I was unsure how far I had traveled with the cold numbing my feet, the snow blowing into my face and stinging my cheeks. Only a few cars passed by at that hour, but a couple of those slowed suspiciously and terrified me. I tried to stick close to the shadows, but it seemed every time that the headlights found me, wrapped around me, pulled me into the open.

I wondered how long Karen and Davies had lingered in my apartment after my departure, and it struck me that it was quite possible that Davies had passed out and was still there. I considered how I had done so much to remove all things political from my life. Even in my work as a hydrologist I seldom involved myself in the use of my findings for any kind of agenda promotion; rather I saw myself as an objective, hired gun. If the state wanted me to study an area for Fish and Game, then I would do it just as quickly as I would respond to the Naturalists' Conservancy's request that I provide a profile for their case against the opening of a region for grazing or recreational use. Terrace formation and sediment evaluation were simple, observable things and meant only what they meant. I didn't talk about politics, didn't respond to talk about politics, didn't care about what I read in the papers, and didn't feel any guilt about my lack of participation in those issues of social importance. I did not know or associate with many black people. As it was, I didn't associate with many people at all, trying at most turns to avoid humans, having in some way taken my grandfather's missing step—complete removal. I didn't need Christianity to dismiss people and I didn't need them to be white.

I simply dismissed them all, quietly, without judgment, equally. I didn't believe in god, I didn't believe in race, and I especially didn't believe in America. I simply didn't care, wouldn't care, refused to care. I was attempting to reconcile this with my new, if accidental, involvement with the American Indian Revolution and my need to understand what was going on. As I crossed under the freeway I realized that my desire to know more was not driven by a fear of the consequences for my having lied to FBI Special Agent Davies, but by a longstanding, unanswered, personal quest to understand my grandfather.

. . .

To uphold the claim would be to adjudge that the direct operation of the treaty was to materially limit and qualify the controlling authority of Congress in respect to the care and protection of the Indians, and to deprive Congress, in possible emergency, when the necessity might be urgent for a partition and disposal of the tribal lands, of all power to act, if the assent of the Indians could not be obtained.

13

My apartment door was unlocked and all the lights were switched off. I hit the switch of the lamp on the table and looked over to the sofa and saw it was empty, then breathed a bit more easily. I could still, however, smell the perfume of alcohol Davies had been wearing. I went to my desk, opened the file drawer, and fingered through my regionally and chronologically arranged collection of watershed studies until I found my most recent work on the Plata Mountain drainage. I sat there reading and re-reading the flow figures, realizing that something was not right. The flow of Silly Man Creek seemed high. After a look at an earlier report I saw that indeed the flow had been considerably lower a few years earlier, a fact that could have been easily explained away if there had been more snow that year; but a glance at the precipitation figures dismissed that as a cause. What was more disconcerting was the fact that the flow of Dog Creek had diminished that same year. If indeed the precipitation numbers were wrong, then both Silly Man and Dog would have had greater flow. I could tell nothing from the aerial photos accompanying the last study.

. . .

While I waited, I watched as Reskin slipped in and out of consciousness; his muttering was reduced now to a whisper. I looked into his eyes, holding the lids open with my fingers, and I saw the resignation, recognized it. I patted his face, but it had no effect. He just lay there, becoming increasingly limp, drifting futher away.

The police arrived before the ambulance. I had left the door ajar and so they pushed in slowly and found me pressing a wet cloth to Reskin's forehead. One cop stood by the door while the other one walked over and started taking the man's pulse. The standing cop pulled out his pad and asked questions.

"What's his name?"

"James Reskin."

"Your name?"

"Robert Hawks."

"Relation?"

"He's just an acquaintance. He's actually my ex-girlfriend's father." I didn't like the way that sounded.

"Ex-girlfriend?"

I nodded, rubbing my face. I watched as Reskin lost consciousness completely. "Yes. He's from Santa Fe. He just showed up here tonight. He seemed kind of depressed and then he pulled this out." I took the pistol from my pocket, which elicited immediate and identical reactions from the cops.

They screamed, together, "Gun! Gun! Drop it! Drop it!" while pulling their weapons and pointing them at me. I tossed the gun to the floor, saying, "It's not loaded! It's not mine!"

The cop who had been taking Reskin's pulse picked up the .32 and the other came over to me, pushing me away and saying, "On your stomach, now!"

My face was pressed against the rug as I watched the policeman examine the pistol and there he was: every cop I had seen when I was growing up, hating me, and afraid of me; I was hating them back. He flipped open the chamber and gave it a glance, then shut it. "It's empty," he said.

"The bullets are in the sink," I said.

"Shut up!"

"Mind if I see a couple of badge numbers, assholes?" I said.

I couldn't see the man behind me, but the one holding Reskin's pistol nodded to him with an exasperated expression and he took his foot out of the middle of my back.

"Can I get up?" I asked.

"Okay," one of the them said.

The paramedics came into the room and went directly to Reskin. They took his blood pressure and looked at his eyes and talked on their radio. "What did he take?" one of the paramedics asked me.

"I don't know. I just realized he was acting funny. He was threatening to kill himself with a pistol and then he got woozy." I was still shaking from anger at the behavior of the cops and I wanted to call them pigs, but instead I looked again at Reskin's face. "I called you guys. He passed out just a few minutes ago."

The paramedics went through Reskin's pockets, but found nothing. "Did he have a bag or anything with him?"

"No. He drove here, but I don't even know what his car looks like. It would have New Mexico tags, I guess."

A paramedic tossed Reskin's keys to one of the cops.

The cop looked at them. "A Mercedes, okay. I'll run down and see if I can find it."

"Can you take him to Mercy?" I asked. "I told his daughter you'd be taking him to Mercy."

As they loaded Reskin onto the stretcher, I thought I saw the fingers of his right hand twitch and I reached out and touched his hand as if he were someone I knew and cared about.

. . .

The fallout that occurred after my grandfather's return from Atlanta was difficult for me to understand. The constant telephone threats became routine, although my father didn't allow me to answer the phone for several weeks. The word in the neighborhood was that my grandfather was a hero, a black man who had stood up for what he believed was right, who had stood up for a poor black man in trouble, who had risked everything, his life, his career, and his family to keep "blacker than black" Bunchy Cooke from frying in the chair in the Peach State. Grandfather didn't wear the event as a triumph, however. He fell silent upon his return, spending more time in his room, and then the news came. The State of Virginia was revoking my grandfather's license to practice medicine; he had committed a crime by failing to notify the proper authorities of a gunshot wound. My father and my grandfather never talked about the matter in front of me, but my father told me what was going on.

"Is he okay?" I asked my father. We were sitting in the kitchen at the table eating from a platter of cookies my mother had delivered earlier. "I mean, he's so quiet."

"He'll be all right. Your grandfather is sixty-seven years old. He's been thinking about retiring anyway. He needs a rest."

"Everybody says Grandfather is a hero," I said.

"I guess he is." My father looked out the window at the backyard. "I'm proud of him. I don't know if I would have had the courage to do what he did."

"Are you scared now? I mean with the threats."

My father nodded. "I wish you'd stay at your mother's."

I just shook my head. "I love her and everything, but I'm not comfortable over there." I felt badly saying it and I put my half-eaten cookie back onto the plate.

"It's okay to feel that way, but she loves you."

"I know."

"So, is there anything you want to talk about, Rob? School, or what about girls? How's the girl situation?"

"Everything is fine," I said, seeing in his eyes that all was not fine. I saw the same worry and concern that I had seen only once before, when I was eleven and suffering from the flu—running an extremely high fever for almost a week. It was before I had left my mother's house and he came over and sat all night by my bed. My mother was scared too and snapped at him about not being able to help me; she suggested that his lack of faith was going to lose him a son. As always, he said nothing but just sat by me and read, looking at me frequently and asking if I knew any good jokes.

"Things are going to work out, aren't they? I mean, all this means is that Grandfather will have more time to fish, right?"

He nodded and pulled a cookie from the pile, held it up to the light of the ceiling fixture and examined it. "How does she get every single one to look exactly the same?"

"She prays while they're in the oven," I said.

My father laughed, and we were silent while he ate the cookie. He said, finally, "I want you to be strong, son."

.   .   .

1706—All and every Negro, Indian, mulatto, or mestee bastard child who shall be born of any Negro, Indian, mulatto, or mestee, shall follow the state and Condition of the Mother and be esteemed a slave.

1712—Any Negro or Indian slave, or any other slave can be baptized but is not free.

1712—No Negro, Indian, or mulatto hereafter made free shall enjoy any houses, lands, tenements within the colony.

1740—All Negroes, Indians, mulattoes, or mestizoes and all their issue are absolute slaves, and shall follow the condition of the mother.

.   .   .

I was tired, cold, hungry, and scared about the business with the FBI and AIR. I was also continuing to hang on, in an anxious way, to the fear of having just walked through the streets of outer and inner Denver in the middle of the dark morning hours. Still

I found my gear, my reports on the Plata Mountain drainage, and my grandfather's shotgun and got into my truck to drive to my cabin.

As I left the lights of Denver, morning was creeping slowly into the sky. I recalled Bisset's brief and cryptic claim about the anthrax bomb and other substances possibly being housed up on the mountain. I didn't know what the Indians were planning and how I would fit in, but it was clear that somehow I would. The thought of it bothered me. I believed now that all of my movements were being observed; every flash of headlights in my mirror gave me a start.

.   .   .

I drove my own car to the hospital and walked into the emergency room just behind the gurney that carried Reskin. I offered what information I could at the desk and was yelled at by a fat nurse for knowing nothing about the man's insurance. Nor did I know his address, home phone number, or have any way to reach his wife. I was able to say only that his daughter was on the way. I found a stiffly cushioned chair and waited. In a few minutes Karen was walking through the doors, her coat open, her movements large as if she were making an entrance. She saw me and glided over; her face was exaggeratedly anguished and her voice a bit too loud as she said, "Tell me he's not dead."

"As far as I know, he's not dead," I said.

"What happened?"

"He came to my apartment, complained about you and your mother, played with a gun that I took away from him, and then proceeded to slip into unconsciousness. And here we are." I stood up and began to fasten my jacket. She watched me, frowning. "I don't know your father. This is your business and I'm going home. I'm sorry he's in a bad way."

"You're going to leave me here?"

"Yes. The nurse over at the desk has some questions for you. Insurance and stuff like that."

"You can't just leave me here like this," she said.

"It's a bad idea for me to stay. If you want me to call a friend to come here and be with you, I'll do it. I could call Ellen. I'm sure she'll come."

"Don't you want to know if he's all right?" She looked around as if embarrassed that others might be hearing our conversation. "I mean, he came to you. Of all people, he came to you."

"No," I said. "I can't help him. Karen, I don't know the man. And I really don't want to give you mixed signals. I don't want to be here for you."

"You are heartless, aren't you?"

"I guess so. Would you like me to call anyone for you?"

"No, just get the hell out!"

I walked away and near the door I was caught by the gaze of an old woman with knitting in her lap whose eyes asked me, "Are you going to leave your friend so upset like that?"

The old woman's face was lined and soft and it reminded me of my mother's, the way the wrinkles around her mouth made it seem to turn downward. Her sad expression was gentle, sweet. I paused there, looking at her, not feeling so much embarrassed by my apparent lack of compassion, but as though I had simply forgotten the rules.

I went back and sat in the chair next to Karen, more scared now than I had been when her crazy father had produced the pistol in my apartment.

. . .

My grandfather continued to treat patients. There were older people who, in spite of his disdain for their religious beliefs, would let no other doctor touch them. It was no secret in the community that he was still practicing, but it didn't seem to matter to anyone. Of course, he couldn't and didn't prescribe medicine, although he dispensed quietly what drugs he had stored, and he had no hospital association. He was sad most of the time, although when people would come visit him at the house (he had decided to stay out of the office altogether), he would not show his feelings to them.

"You're going to have to go to Dr. Adams, Mr. Cooper," Grandfather said to the feeble man sitting in the study.

"But I don't know him," Mr. Cooper said, with his large, delicate hands folded together.

"Trust me. You need to be admitted into the hospital and he can do that for you."

"You used to see me in the hospital," the man said.

"Go to Dr. Adams."

"God bless you, Doc Hawks."

"Save it," my grandfather said, waving a hand in the air, and the old man laughed.

Mr. Cooper left and my grandfather remained in the study. He sat with his back to the desk, facing the window and the steel gray sky that promised snow. I went into the room and sat on the sofa.

"Grandfather, what are you going to do now that you're kind of retired?"

He swiveled in the chair and looked at me. "That's essentially the way it is, isn't it? I don't know. I guess I'll get to do a lot more fishing and hunting. What do you think I should do?" As he said it, both he and I watched the early stages of his neurological disorder, his hands quaking there in his lap.

"Fishing and hunting sound good to me," I said.

Grandfather studied me for a long second. "What are you going to be when you're done with school?" he asked me, leaning back and groaning as he put his feet on the desk. He knocked a journal to the floor, but didn't care.

"I'm not going to be a doctor," I said, perhaps just a little too quickly.

He laughed.

"I want to do something outside. I've been reading and I was thinking maybe geology or something like that."

He nodded.

"I don't think I like people enough to be a doctor," I said, hoping to justify my position.

He stared at me for a few seconds, then said, "That sounds right, I guess. I don't like them enough either."

"But you're a good doctor," I told him.

He shrugged. "I've delivered a lot of babies. I've prescribed a lot of antibiotics. You know, Robert, I actually enjoy helping people. Most of my patients never pay me. Can't pay me. Too poor. But that's all right. I don't mind." He looked at the ceiling. "A geologist, eh?"

"Or something like that. I like biology, too."

"I wouldn't have minded a job outside, myself," he said. "I was surprised when your father went into medicine. He's turned out to be a better doctor than me."

"That's not what he says."

"My grandson, the geologist." He smiled at me. Then his smile faded and he said, "Just do something you love. That's really the only thing that matters. Do something you have to do. Find it and do it. Life is too short."

.　.　.

Hear ye Dakotas. Yet before the ashes of the council fire are cold, the Great Father is building his forts among us. You have heard the sound of the white soldiers' axes upon the Little Piney. His presence here is

an insult and a threat. It is an insult to the spirits of our ancestors. Are
we to give up their sacred grounds to be plowed for corn? Dakotas, I am
for war.

·   ·   ·

Halfway to Plata I hit a patch of black ice on a bridge that sent the
truck skidding, my lights catching the white-and-gray guard rail a
fraction of a second before my bumper. I skated along the rail, trying to regain control by turning the wheel in the direction of the
spin as I had been taught, my foot off the brake. Suddenly the
truck seemed to correct itself, until I hit the dry pavement and
then the truck was twisted into a spin in the opposite direction
and I found myself sliding sideways through the slush and snow
of the median strip. It happened so quickly and yet so slowly, and
although I didn't see my life or any portion of it flash by, I did
hear my grandfather's voice, saying nothing in particular, just his
voice. It wasn't until I was motionless in the middle of the center
divider that I could make out what my grandfather was saying. It
was from a time when we were hunting wild hogs, when we had
to run from a large boar that had sneaked up behind us. We were
swinging to and fro in the skinny cypress trees we had scrambled
up, with the hog angrily clicking his tusks down on the ground,
and he said, "Don't you feel alive, Robert?"

·   ·   ·

I switched off the truck's engine and sat there for a while. My head
had banged against the driver's-side window, but the glass was
still intact and, as far as I could ascertain, so was I. I was scared to
death and I asked myself questions to see whether I was okay, like
what day it was and where was I and what kind of truck did I have
and what was my mother's maiden name. Then it occurred to me
that if I actually was suffering from a concussion, I would not be

able to distinguish right from wrong answers and, further, that what I thought made so much sense might indeed be utter nonsense. And the more I thought about making sense, the more I became convinced that my thinking was tortured, probably because of some brain trauma. In the early morning light, with a snow flurry bothering my windshield, I restarted my truck and got it going in the right direction.

.   .   .

They pumped Reskin's stomach and he did not die immediately. That was the upshot. Edith Reskin flew up and arrived early the next morning. She took a cab from the airport and joined us at the hospital. I waited while she and her daughter went into the intensive care unit for the few minutes they allowed and gawked helplessly at the man's pallid, voiceless body. Mrs. Reskin remained at the hospital and Karen asked me if I'd take her home for a change of clothes.

On the way, Karen reached over and touched my hand, her gaze directed forward through the windshield. "Robert, I want to thank you for everything you've done. I wouldn't have made it through this without you."

I said nothing. I stopped the car at a red light and turned up the heat. I checked the fuel gauge and the temperature of the engine and the battery gauge, then I turned on the radio and found some news on an AM station.

"Why do you think my father came to you?" Karen asked, staring at me.

I shrugged.

"I think it's because he sees in you what I see in you."

"What's that?" The light changed and I moved the truck forward with the traffic.

"Strength."

I glanced into the mirror at my own eyes and all I saw was fear. "You think that's it, eh? Well, I pretty much think your father is certifiable."

"He's a very intense man."

"Yeah, you could call it that."

I parked in front of her duplex and wanted very much to wait in the truck, but she insisted that I come in; she said that it was too cold to be outside, that she needed me close by. We walked to the door and I had to help her with the key in the lock.

"It's been sticking a lot lately," she said.

"I'll take a look at it while you change." And it all felt awful. I was standing there squirting WD-40 from the can I kept in the truck into the lock mechanism of Karen's front door, waiting for her to climb back into my truck and tell me how close we were and how much she needed me and on and on.

She called to me.

"Yes?"

"Could you come here please?"

I walked through the living room and to the doorway of the bedroom. "What is it?" And then I saw her and she was butt-naked and standing on the bed, bouncing up and down on her toes.

"What are you doing?" I asked.

She flopped down into a sitting position and stared at me. "I need you, Robert."

I wanted to cry. "Come on, get dressed so we can get back to the hospital. I've got to go to work today."

"Call in sick. Tell them a relative is in the hospital." She lay back and said, "Take me."

There was a sadness deep in her face and I found that somehow I did care about her feelings. I didn't want to hurt Karen. I had never wanted to hurt Karen. I went and sat on the bed beside her. "Karen," I said, "this is not the right time. I mean, we can talk about it later. I promise. But right now you need to go to the hospital and be with your mother."

"I'm so scared," she said. She reached up and hugged me around my neck.

"I know."

She was crying softly now. I raked the tears from her face with my fingers. "Listen, he's going to be all right. The doctor was confident about that."

And then she was kissing me. I kissed her back. Her tongue opened my mouth and I could taste her tears now, and her body became soft and her eyes stayed shut behind fluttering lids, and I was pathetically willing as her hands found me and my hands found her.

.   .   .

At my cabin, the side of my head was still hurting, but I felt fairly sure that I had not been seriously injured. I put on thermal underwear, neoprene socks, and my waterproof boots and collected my snowshoes, first-aid kit, light, and the shotgun that had been my grandfather's. I got into my truck and drove around past the lake and up the mountain as far as I could. There I got out and followed Dog Creek.

The hiking was relatively easy at first, as the new snow had blown and drifted in a way that left a good deal of usable trail. I hadn't been up there for a long time, as I usually chose to fish Hell-hole Creek, which was near my place. But I could tell, even in its frozen state, that something was wrong. The whole of the flow was frozen, not just the sides, and I knew that it hadn't been cold enough to freeze the Dog Creek I remembered, but this was a trickle. The fact that I hadn't slept and that I was nearly killed on the highway began to catch up with me. My muscles were aching. My head hurt. My vision seemed to be getting blurry, which didn't settle my worries about a concussion. I stopped, leaned against an aspen, and ate one of the candy bars I had brought with me, but it was terribly unsatisfying and only reminded me that I couldn't remember my last meal.

I walked for about two and a half hours and then I saw it and I couldn't believe it. There, in the middle of nowhere on Dog Creek, was a dam, a real honest-to-goodness poured-concrete dam, and the gate of it did not open into the Dog, but instead led down the mountain in a direction ninety degrees opposed to it.

I sat on the wall of the dam and looked at it. It was an expert job. Certainly no campers had come up and built it in a weekend. Beavers weren't the cause—they have no facility with concrete. The raised pipeline that led away was eighteen inches in diameter, big enough to accommodate the heaviest flows of the Dog in spring. The gate was shut, and I could see down the line that plugs had been removed from the bottom and dangled at the ends of chains. The pipeline had been opened to allow a complete discharge so that water wouldn't freeze and rupture the steel. This was some piece of engineering. I forgot how tired and hungry I was and began to trace the pipe through the forest. The shotgun was becoming heavy and I moved it from side to side as I walked. The line went about a mile, over a couple of arroyos, and opened onto a hillside, then it just stopped. I studied the land there, the terracing, looking up toward the tree line and down the mountain and then it hit me. Here the drainage was into the Silly Man Creek. I was in Silly Man Canyon and from here the water would feed down into the Plata, which ran through the Plata Creek Indian Reservation and not into Hellhole Lake, which held water for both Indian and non-Indian ranchers.

. . .

There is no one who has been a close observer of Indian history and the effect of contact of Indians with civilization, who is not well satisfied that one of two things must eventually take place, to wit, either civilization or extermination of the Indian. Savage and civilized life cannot live and prosper on the same ground. One of the two must die. If the Indians are to be civilized and become a happy and prosperous people, which is certainly the object and intention of our Government, they must learn our language and adopt our modes of life. We are fifty millions of people, and they are only one-fourth of one million. The few must yield to the many.

.   .   .

It had been raining on and off all day and the evening had turned quite cold. My father and I were unwrapping after having taken a post-dinner walk. As my father took my coat to hang up in the closet, Grandfather came into the foyer. "They shot Dr. King," he said, as he turned and walked away back into the study. My father finished hanging up my jacket, and put his hat on the shelf, and closed the closet door. He didn't look at me, nor did I see in his face any expression that might give me a clue as to what to feel. He followed Grandfather's steps into the study and I followed his, and we sat in front of the television watching the news. My grandfather's hand was tapping the armrest of his chair in a frantic rhythm, but it wasn't his Parkinson's. It was 4 April 1968, and I had school the next day.

.   .   .

At the diner next to Clara's store, I sat at the counter in front of a plate of scrambled eggs and bacon with a side of buckwheat pancakes and listened to Laurel tell a woman with long red hair how she wasn't going to marry a pig like a certain Mr. Wood, but she would continue to go by the name Laurel because she liked it.

A newspaper was on the seat beside me and I picked it up, put it on the counter next to my plate. One of the sub-headlines of the front page read, "Custer's Remains Stolen." I read the story. The grave at Little Bighorn Monument believed to contain the body of General George Armstrong Custer had been dug up and emptied by *parties unknown*.

My back was slapped in that friendly sort of way that I really hate and I turned to find young Deputy Hanson sliding onto the stool beside me.

"It's a little late for breakfast, ain't it?" he asked, a big cowboy smile painting his face.

I looked at my watch and saw it was eight o'clock and then out at the darkness. "Oh, it's eight P.M.," I said.

Hanson laughed. "What you been up to?"

"I was in Denver for a few days," I told him. "What do you know new?"

"Nothing much. Somebody's been shoplifting food from Clara's. That's about it for major crime. I wrote a ticket today and cleaned a dog's guts off the highway." He looked at my food. "Sorry."

Laurel came down the counter and wiped the counter in front of Hanson. "Coffee?"

"Yeah, and one of the those doughnuts." He pointed to the pastries under a glass cover. "And give me one of the fresh ones with a lot of glaze on it."

"Aren't you afraid of becoming a cliché?" I asked.

"I ain't scared of nothing."

Laurel filled the deputy's cup with coffee and slid a small plate with a doughnut on it in front of him. He thanked her and she went back to her friend.

"What do you hear about the FBI men?" I asked.

Hanson shook his head while he set down his cup. "It's like

it never happened. There were more questions and cops crawling around here measuring stuff after that big rig wreck last year." He took an exceptionally large bite of doughnut and continued with a full mouth. "You hear anything else from them state cops?"

"Nope." I pushed my eggs around my plate a little. "Just that one visit."

"They sure didn't like you very much." He laughed and poured some black coffee into his face. "Of course, you didn't give 'em any reason to."

"I guess not."

"You hear about the trouble down in Plata?"

I shook my head. "What kind of trouble?"

"Some troopers chased a speeder onto the rez and got into a shoot-out with some Indians. They shot a guy named Wallace Crow Feather. Guy wasn't even a Plata, but from South Dakota someplace. They shot him dead."

"When did this happen?" I asked.

"Real early this morning."

"Fifty-five, stay alive," I said.

Hanson laughed loudly, consuming his last bite. "That's a good one. I'm going to tell that one." He slid off the stool and pushed himself away from the counter. "Gotta roll." He called down a good-bye to Laurel and gave me another slap on the back.

. . .

In Clara's I bought my usual milk along with some eggs, bread, and fruit. Clara was sharpening pencils with a pocket knife behind the counter when I came up.

"I hear you've been having some thefts," I said, setting the stuff on the counter.

"Yeah, and if I catch the stinking son-of-a-bitch I'm going to string his sorry rear end from a high tree," she said. "I don't like being stole from. Even if it's a jelly bean."

"Especially the red ones."

"Damn straight." She figured my total. "By the way, you got a call here this morning. From that Davies woman, you know, the one from the FBI."

"Thanks," I said.

"You gonna call her back?"

"I'll call her later," I said. I put my goods in the paper sack she'd set on the counter.

"You in some kind of trouble?"

"No," I said. "Not yet."

.   .   .

What I felt as I sat behind the wheel of my truck as I drove back up the mountain to my cabin was unclear. If indeed the investigation of the murders of the FBI men was only half-hearted, a mere token, and I was leaning toward believing it—the only agent who had talked to me was the drunken Davies, after all—then I really didn't have to worry much about having lied about seeing Louise Yellow Calf. Well, I thought that for a second, and then extreme fear of the consequences of the lie returned. I had come to terms, more or less, with why I had lied, but consideration of the possible problems that might arise left my stomach feeling cold and hollow, and pushed back toward my spine. But added now to my sick, icy fear was the annoying curiosity that had been aroused by my discovery of the dam and pipeline in the woods. I couldn't begin to guess who had made it or how they had made it without attracting at least a small amount of attention, without building a road. I was going back up the mountain to look around, above the dam and pipeline, up to the top. As I looked through the windshield up at the sky I realized that the weather was not going to cooperate with me. I also knew I was stupid enough to let impatience get the better of me, that I wouldn't be able to let the simple major winter storm that was brewing finish with the landscape before I began my climb.

14

I read in the paper about the riots in Washington and Chicago and saw the burning buildings on television, and I wondered whether anything was going to happen in Richmond. There were a lot of police cars driving through the neighborhood as I walked home from school the day following the assassination. The cops stared at me and I stared back. I wondered why, at one hundred thirty pounds, I scared them so much. I felt the wrinkle in my forehead between my eyes grow deep like my father's and grandfather's. The cops wanted me to look away, to walk faster or slower, to run home, to be affected by them, to be worried that they saw me—but I wasn't worried, I wanted them to see me, I wanted them to see me staring at them, to see me hating them. My mother called and asked me to stay around the house and not go out. I got mad at her and when she insisted, I yelled at her to leave me alone. My father heard me and told me to call back and apologize and I shouted, "No!" and ran out of the house. I was on fire and I didn't know why. I sat on the corner three blocks away and waved to the police cars. Five or six other guys and I just waved at them and mouthed the words "Fuck you." It all felt so necessary, so necessary and so empty and unsatisfying.

.   .   .

Bunchy Cooke was shot in the back of the head twice by .38 caliber slugs fired from two different police service revolvers. The projectiles passed through the occipital bone into the occipital lobe, across the parieto-occipital fissure, through the parietal

173

lobe, and lodged in the limbic lobe above the corpus callosum. The second one traveled just a bit farther and came to rest in the calloso-marginal fissure. Bunchy Cooke died on some street in Atlanta while an ambulance was detained at the police blockade. My grandfather no longer practiced medicine. Bunchy Cooke no longer walked among the living.

. . .

In regard to the Black Hills, I look upon it as very important to the Indians to make some treaty by which, if gold is discovered in large quantities, the white people will be allowed to go there, and they receive a full equivalent for all that is rendered.

If gold is not found there in large quantities, of course the white people won't for the present want to go there, and their country will be left as it is now.

. . .

To say the least, fucking Karen again was a bad idea. To say the most, it was perhaps the stupidest thing any single individual had ever done in the history of human interaction. She screamed and claimed her orgasm was the most intense she had ever had and lay there with her eyes closed saying that she was sure that it was an omen that we were back together for good, that her father would live, and she would thank him for being the cause of our profound happiness. I sat on the edge of the bed pulling on my trousers, shaking my head, wanting to cry, wanting to leap through the window. But instead I said, "We've got to get back to the hospital. Your mother needs you."

Dressed, we made the drive back to the hospital and Karen asked, while I parked in the lot beside a huge mound of snow, "Why do you think my father is so unhappy?"

I shrugged.

"I don't know what he expects from life. I never have known. I think he hates me. Isn't that terribly sad? Do you think my father hates me?"

I opened my door to get out, but I answered, "Yes."

"Why?"

I was out now and my door was closed. Karen got out and walked around the truck to catch up with me as I walked toward the entrance of the hospital. She took my arm as we entered.

"Why do you think he hates me?" she asked, sounding distraught, but then she always sounded distraught, and when I looked at her I saw that her blue eyes were welling up.

.   .   .

My grandfather and I were driving home after a day out searching for wild pigs that didn't want to be found. We drove through the dark countryside quietly; my grandfather was humming while I looked out my window at the silhouettes of trees. I saw the lights as the car began to slow and all of a sudden we were in the middle of it. Two men cloaked in flowing white and wearing conical white hoods directed the slowing traffic while off in the field behind them similarly dressed men made an impressive crowd around a burning cross. I could tell my grandfather wanted to step on the gas and speed past, but there were cars immediately ahead of us and the opposite lane was filled with traffic, which made it impossible to turn about. The klansmen were peering into the cars ahead of us as they rolled by, but all of those drivers and passengers were white. I was shaking, but I wanted to shout, wanted to shout that they were walking assholes, that they were ignorant cowards, that they were pigs, but I didn't. I sank into the seat of my grandfather's Oldsmobile and tried to breathe normally. The hooded white face leaned close to my grandfather's window and the man called for the attention of his partner who looked in, too. They started to shout "nigger" at us and kick at the car. That's when I noticed the pistol in my grandfather's lap. It was the .22 target pistol he had once let me fire at tin cans at a man's farm in Hopper. He had it full in his hand now, his finger on the trigger. Then the car in front of us accelerated to speed on down the highway and my grandfather bolted after him. Just as quickly as the pistol had appeared in his lap, it was gone. He smiled at me, sweat on his aging brow. He resumed his humming and I peered out the window at the silhouettes of trees.

.   .   .

This time when I went up the mountain I took my camera. The ambient temperature that morning was considerably lower than it had been earlier, a warning of the bad weather coming. I had my tent and my stove with me, since I thought I might have to wait out the blizzard. The snow was just beginning to fall as I reached the dam on Dog Creek. I took pictures of the dam and the pipeline.

I continued on along the Dog, and noticed that the creek looked more normal above the dam. The snow fell more heavily as the temperature plummeted. Ice formed in my mustache and I cinched the hood of my parka more tightly about my head. I knew it was cold but I couldn't feel it; I was too excited and scared. Finally, though, I couldn't see the stream bed for the snow coming down, nor could I see very far in front of me. The blizzard was full on and it was everything it had promised it would be. I set up my tent, crawled in, got off my wet clothes, put on dry ones, lit my pocket hand-warmers, and slid into my sleeping bag.

.   .   .

Two adjacent streams might drain to the same base level and form on the mountain front on the alluvial fan above the adjacent inter-fan stream that heads at the front. It is the case, however, that the low-gradient inter-fan stream cannot carry the coarse alluvium, and when it is arrested by an adjacent stream, an active aggradational phase begins.

. . .

Edith Reskin was beside herself, pacing and saying things like, "Where is his god now?" and "I hope he doesn't have a vision or a revelation or something like that." Karen and I stood near her for nearly half a minute before she noticed us. She looked at me. "Can you imagine having to listen to him if he has a near-death experience?" Edith Reskin cried.

"What is it, Mother?" Karen asked. "What's wrong? Mother?"

"He's dying." Edith Reskin sniffed and tried to catch her breath. She was patting her hair absently as if getting ready for a picture.

"The doctors said he's going to be all right," Karen said, starting to cry now with her mother.

Edith Reskin was shaking her head. "That's not what they're saying now. He's conscious, but everything is slowing down."

"What are they saying?"

"He's dying and they don't know why. They say they don't understand."

Karen and her mother went into the room to see Reskin. I sat on the square sofa in the waiting area and read a couple of magazines. Before long Karen and her mother were standing in front of me and one of them was saying, "He wants to talk to you."

I just looked at them.

"He wants you," Karen said.

"Well, I'm not going in there." I crossed my legs and looked out the window.

"Please," Edith Reskin said. "Please."

I got up and Edith Reskin embraced me and I felt just how small a woman she was. I placed my hand flat against her back and gave her a pat. She was so fragile there, so unlike the woman who had always stood up to the monster Reskin. I wondered about her grief at that moment, wondered just where was the man with whom she had fallen in love. Certainly, the difficult, born-again, self-righteous, self-centered man lying on the bed in the other room was not that man, but she still loved him, or loved what he had been. Maybe it wasn't love at all, but some sick clinging to the past, an avoidance of the realization of a loss that had already happened.

.   .   .

I walked into the room and saw Reskin lying in the bed; the rhythm of his body was being monitored by the machine at his bedside. I had expected to find him intubated, but his face was free of apparatus. He raised a weak hand when I got to his bed, but I didn't take it and so it fell idle beside his body.

"They tell me you're dying," I said.

He nodded.

"I guess that's what you want, though."

"It is," he whispered.

Neither of us spoke for a long couple of minutes. I was looking out the window at the clouds and wondering how long protocol would have me stay.

"Find it for me," he said.

"Find what?"

"Find a reason," he said.

I wasn't interested in what he had to say to me. I was just there, but as I stood looking at his crazy eyes, I knew why he was dying. It was so simple and I knew that there was no cure. He was dying because he wanted to. Not because he had resigned, not because he had given up, but because he wanted to die: he had willed it and was mean enough to carry it through.

I said to him, "So, nobody pays enough attention to you. Is that it?"

"Don't be afraid," he said.

"Afraid of what?"

"Just don't be afraid. That's why you're with my daughter who isn't good enough for you. You're afraid. Don't be scared, Robert."

"I'm not afraid."

He smiled. Then he stopped smiling and closed his eyes, and he died right there in front of me, with a tiny pathetic, high-pitched gasp. The line of the machine went flat and caused an alarm to sound.

.   .   .

The snow stopped at some point during the night. I pushed out of my tent through the drift and looked at the blanketed landscape. The white was like a whisper across the mountain; everything was so hushed, so motionless. I cooked some dehydrated eggs on my stove and felt my body warm up as I ate. I tried to get my bearings when I realized I could see the top of the mountain. What I also saw was an unnatural clearing some hundred yards away. It was near the tree line, so I knew immediately why I hadn't detected it in the aerial photographs. I left my camp intact and walked to the clearing. Aspens were downed and pushed to the sides in an area that must have been thirty yards square. I tripped over something under the snow, then, kneeling and brushing through, I found a dead elk. It was a big bull and its face, the glassy eyes hollow and still alive-looking, startled me a little and disturbed me greatly. I fell back a couple of steps, then turned away from the sight. I observed the middle of the clearing and saw that the snow was thinning there, melting evenly across the surface; the center was already crusting over, just like snow looks over a septic tank. I took out my camera and snapped pictures of the clearing and of the dead elk, then marked the spot on my map.

．　．　．

My heart is glad that some of my people who have died have been so well taken care of and buried on scaffolds. When I get back to my people I will tell them what you have done. I would like to have some things to take back to them. There are three things that I have always been against. Last fall, when I was here, I spoke about it. I want to be sure that the goods you are giving us are presents and not annuity goods. We do not want any treaty goods from you at all. These whites that you have put in my buffalo country I despise and I want to see them away. I suppose your great father sent you here to tell me that I am going to live. What you are talking about—signing the treaty—I do not want to do. I cannot do anything here by myself. You know very well that if the treaty is signed by only a portion of our people it is not likely to stand. When Red Cloud and Man Afraid of His Horses come in, whatever they do I am willing to do the same.

．　．　．

When I tried to get some sleep upon returning home, I was troubled by a dream. In it, a rust-brown bull elk staggered across a pristine mountain meadow surrounded by graceful aspens, with knot eyes all gazing outward. The meadow was striking, covered with penstemon and mariposa tulips sticking their yellow faces toward the sun, and with spurred lupines. The hooves of the elk fell heavily among the flowers and I walked toward it, but it didn't notice me, it couldn't notice me. I recognized the glassy empty eyes and I realized that the eyes stuck into the bark of the aspens seemed more alive than the elk's eyes. I was crying in the dream, following the zig-zagging path of the elk. I looked at the clear blue sky and thought what a beautiful day it was, how warm and glorious, and I found my feet falling effortlessly into the tracks of the elk. I staggered with him, my shoulders slumping, my breathing beginning to race. I felt my heart hot in my chest. And then I was outside of myself and looking into my own big, glassy elk eyes.

The next few days went by slowly at my cabin. Although I'd had no visitors, I was anxious. The road, and especially the snow-packed lane to my house, no doubt discouraged travel to my place, but the constant sun since the last storm was cleaning things up. I expected the authoritative or drunken knocking of Davies or the frantic clawing of Karen at my door at any second. My appetite was off and so I could make it through a couple more days without a trip down to Clara's. A knock did finally come, but it was tentative and didn't sound urgent.

When I opened the door I found Hiram and Dicky Kills Enemy standing there. I let them in.

"It's nice and warm in here, Robert," Hiram said, sitting by the stove.

Dicky remained standing, like a sentry by the door.

"To what do I owe this pleasure?" I asked, sitting on a stool at the counter. "Would you like some tea?"

Hiram shook his head. He looked around the room. "You don't have a television."

"Nope."

"Radio?" Hiram asked.

I shook my head, laughing. "Why?"

"So, you haven't heard."

I sat up straight and looked at him. "Heard what?"

"Tyrone, Louise, the Hat boys, and a bunch of others are holed up in the Saint Luke compound."

"What do you mean, 'holed up'?" I asked.

Hiram looked over at Dicky. "How would you describe it, Grandson?"

"They're locked in. The Feds are locked out. Everybody's got guns. Everybody's shooting." Dicky's face showed no emotion, but he looked directly at me while he spoke.

"What happened?"

Hiram looked tired and suddenly old. "We found out about their mess up on the mountain. We don't know where it is, but we know it's there and we know what they're trying to do to us."

I didn't say anything.

"That Indian FBI and that other black one tried to tell us, but they killed them," Hiram said.

"Anthrax?" I asked. "That's what Bisset said."

Hiram shrugged.

"I know where it is," I said. "I found it."

Hiram and Dicky just stared at me.

"I think I found it. I took pictures of it, a couple of rolls. I found a dam. If there was a leak, it would normally drain into Dog Creek. What they've done is divert the flow of the Dog to the Silly Man and right onto the reservation." I grabbed my topographical map from the counter, unfolded it, and walked over to Hiram. "It's right here. Up high, almost to the tree line."

"It's bad over there," Dicky said. "They need food and the roads are all blocked."

Hiram said, "They're going to stay there until the government admits what they're doing."

The question of who cared if Indians were sleeping in a church on the reservation must have been obvious on my face, because Dicky said, "They've got two hostages. Two FBIs."

"Oh my god."

"Yes, indeed," Hiram said.

"I need you to get me across the mountain," Dicky said. "It's the only way to get supplies through to them. You know the way. You can get me in behind the Feds."

I rubbed a hand over my face and looked at the two men. Hiram was staring at me, but he wasn't begging.

"How bad is it?" I asked.

Dicky shook his head. "They've got soldiers and a tank and it's a mess, a real mess."

I walked over to the counter and spread open the map. "Okay, Dicky, come show me where the church is."

. . .

It took a while for me to understand James Reskin's last words, and whether he was making sense or not was unimportant, as the sense I found was mine. I stayed with Karen after her father's death because I was afraid to hurt her at a time like that, at least that was the lie I told myself. I had a brief feeling of being un-needed. It was sick and quiet and insidious, and once I'd isolated and identified it, it was undeniable and then embarrassing. Karen was, without question, crazy, but no more to blame, even less so, than I. She was a lunatic with whom I had to deal, but I was the problem. Months after her father's death, I understood. I wasn't afraid anymore.

"Why?!" she screamed, her voice much louder than her size. "Because you need to get away from me? Am I that awful?"

"No, I'm going up there because I want to go fishing. I like fishing. It relaxes me."

"And I don't relax you?!"

"Karen," I said. "Sit down, please." I waited until she was seated and looked at her eyes from across the room. "Karen, I keep tell-ing you that I care about you and in some way I guess that's true. But it's also not quite true. We're in this sick thing together and I want out. Let me change that—I'm getting out." She was stunned, sitting there, playing with her fingers in her lap. "We don't have a relationship, Karen. I don't love you. I have never loved you. I will never love you. I'm sorry. Now, if you'll excuse me, I'm going fishing."

I got her to her feet and nudged her to the door, where she said, just as I was closing it, "Okay, darling, I'll talk to you later."

. . .

Article 13. The tribe herein named, by their representatives, parties to this treaty, agree to make the reservation herein described their permanent home, and they will not as a tribe make any settlement elsewhere, reserving the right to hunt the lands adjoining the said reservation formerly called theirs, subject to the modifications named in this treaty and the orders of the commander of the department in which said reservation may be for the time being; and it is further agreed and understood by the parties to this treaty, that if any Indian or Indians shall leave the reservation herein to settle elsewhere, he or they shall forfeit all the rights, privileges, and annuities conferred by the terms of this treaty; and it is further agreed by the parties to this treaty, that they will do all they can to induce Indians now away from reservations set apart for the exclusive use and occupation of the Indians, leading a nomadic life, or engaged in war against the people of the United States, to abandon such a life and settle permanently in one of the territorial reservations set apart for the exclusive use and occupation of the Indians.

. . .

Dicky Kills Enemy came back to my house later that day alone with two large pea green canvas packs filled with food staples. "You know, food is really heavy," he said, putting the bags down with a thud on the floor just inside the door. Snow melted off his black leather boots. "How long will it take to get there? What is it, like twenty miles?" He wore a semiautomatic .45 pistol strapped to his side.

I wanted to get going as quickly as possible, as I didn't know whether Davies would be showing up, drunk or otherwise, and I felt anxious to get underway before good sense returned and I changed my mind. I lifted one of the bags in a test and groaned, then set it back down. "With this load, it might take us most of the day."

Dicky nodded.

I tossed an extra pair of snowshoes to him, one at a time. "You ever use those?" I asked.

"No." He examined them, tracing the wood and sinew with his finger.

"It's not too hard. We might need them. We might not." I pulled two lighter weight, nylon backpacks from my closet and tossed them to the floor by the food. "Why don't you divide the food between those two bags," I said.

"Repack it?"

"Those bags are lighter and they won't get soaked like the canvas ones."

Dicky understood and set to work quickly. I collected my map and my compass and my shotgun, and shoved a bunch of shells into the pockets of my parka. Then I stopped and my stopping must have been conspicuous because Dicky looked at me and asked what was wrong.

"Nothing," I said, taking the red, plastic-cased shells from my coat and putting them on the counter. I unloaded the shotgun and leaned it against the wall by the refrigerator.

"You're not taking the gun?" Dicky asked.

"Too heavy."

Dicky didn't question me, just continued loading the packs.

"Personally, I didn't think you would help us, but my grandfather said you would. He likes you. He's never wrong about people."

"What about you? Do you like me?"

"I don't know," Dicky said. "Do *you* like *me*? I usually like people who like me." Finished with packing the food, he sat on the floor and watched as I retied my boots. He looked at the cabin walls, at the couple of photographs of birds I had hanging, and scratched his head. "Tell me, why are you helping us?"

"I wasn't planning on it, I can tell you that." I grabbed my gloves from the kitchen counter. "At first I was just curious, I guess, about Louise, about what had happened to the FBI men and, all of a sudden, I was involved, because of my own stupidity, but involved. I couldn't seem to help that part."

"But now?"

"Now, I know there's something bad wrong on the mountain. If there is the kind of shit Bisset and your grandfather think is up there, then we could be talking about murder."

"You can't murder Indians," Dicky said.

"What?"

"Murder is a legal concept. You can kill an Indian, but you can't murder one. You've got to have a law against it before it's murder."

. . .

Article XIII. All animosities for past grievances shall henceforth cease; and the contracting parties will carry the foregoing treaty into full execution, with all good faith and sincerity.

. . .

It was sunny out and we walked with our jackets open. Dicky Kills Enemy was in better shape than I had been in some time, but luckily I was in the lead and so controlled our pace. He hardly seemed to feel the climb when I had to take my first rest.

"You work out?" I asked.

"A little. Remember, I'm probably ten years younger than you are," he said.

"I'll try to keep that in mind." I slipped my arms from the straps of the pack of food I was carrying and sat on it. "We're almost to the dam I told you about."

Dicky lit a filterless cigarette and let the smoke come back through his nose; he pushed the match out in the snow.

Still breathing hard, I said, "You know smoking's not good for your lungs."

"Yeah, I know. I've been trying to quit."

We sat quietly for a minute or so, then Dicky chuckled to himself.

"What?" I asked.

"There was this Plata boy who asked his father how we Indians get our names. The boy's father said, 'Son, when your sister was born, I looked out the teepee and saw that the moon was yellow like corn and so we named her Yellow Moon. And when your brother was born I looked out and saw a young elk run through our camp and so we called him Swift Elk. And when your baby brother was born I looked out and there was a bad storm coming, so we call him Storms Quickly. But tell me, why do you ask, Two Dogs Fucking?'"

I laughed at the old joke and I could see that Dicky had enjoyed hearing himself tell it.

"How'd you meet up with Bisset?" I asked.

"We were in college together. The University of New Mexico. We were Lobos."

"So, what happened? You drop out?"

"Tyrone did. I finished. American Studies, so-called. I want to go to law school. John Hat and I graduated together."

I pulled a couple of candy bars from my pocket and offered one to Dicky. He took it and unwrapped it, then turned it over to look at the package.

"I just want to be sure there's no coconut in this," he said. "I hate coconut."

"Allergic?"

"No, I just hate it. The texture of it, you know?"

We sat for a while longer and when I felt ready, I stood up and got the pack situated on my back. "I don't mind telling you that I'm scared enough to turn back any time now," I said.

Dicky nodded and I could see that he was scared, too.

. . .

At the dam, Dicky let out a low whistle. "This is some piece of work," he said. "When you said dam, I thought you meant like a bunch of sticks and rocks, like a beaver dam or something." He whistled again. Then he saw the pipeline stretching away as far as we could see. "I don't get it."

I pointed up the mountain. "Somebody doesn't want to contaminate the lake with whatever's up there. But apparently they don't give a shit about Indians." I stood and grabbed my load, a little angrier and more determined to get to the compound. "Let's get going."

. . .

. . . it is possible, in the name of the Holy Trinity, to send all the slaves which it is possible to sell . . . of whom, if the information which I have is correct, they tell me that one can sell 4,000. . . . And, certainly, the information seems authentic, because in Castile and Portugal and

*Aragon and Italy and Sicily and the islands of Portugal and Aragon
and the Canaries they utilize many slaves, and I believe that those from
Guinea are not now enough. . . . In any case there are these slaves and
brazilwood, which seem a profitable thing, and still gold.*

. . .

Grandfather was staring out the window at a young couple passing the house. It was a warm, spring day, which offered a small
assembly of clouds in the southwest. I could see the clouds over
the trees as I gazed out the window with him.

"Where's Dad?" I asked.

"He has a meeting at noon."

"Are you okay, Grandfather?"

"I'm tired, Robert." He looked at his hands and rubbed the
tips of his quavering fingers against his thumbs. "Some people
just seem to live day-to-day and nothing gets to them. They get
jobs, lose jobs, have babies, bury babies. And they just keep going."
He shook his head and took a deep breath. "Hey, you want to go
see if we can find us a pig? We can go out for a couple of hours and
be back before dinner."

"I don't know if we should go hunting," I said. "I don't think
it's a good idea."

"It's a great idea, Robert," he said. "It's the right idea."

"Looks like rain."

"So? What's a little rain?"

. . .

It was well after nightfall when Dicky and I topped the ridge
behind the little church; the hike had taken less time than I had
estimated. The whole compound was lit up like daytime from big
floodlights surrounding it. The clear night was exceptionally cold

and I shivered, and pulled up my hood and cinched it. There were soldiers and cops and armed cowboys everywhere to the south and east of the church. There was an armored personnel carrier parked about a hundred yards away from the building, about three hundred yards from us. There was brush all the way down the hill to the church, the kind of dense brush that in the summer would shelter snakes, and the light didn't illuminate the north side as brightly. Still, I didn't want to go down. I had pretty much made up my mind not to, and was about to tell Dicky that I had gotten him this far and now he was on his own, when the sound of footsteps crunching through the snow and the sight of flashlight beams sweeping the darkness behind us sent the two of us crawling, packs on our backs, pushing into the wet cold of the ground. We made noise, the cans rattling in our packs, and the lights washed over the brush all around us as we scrambled along on our bellies. We were nearly to the rear doors of the church when I saw a beam of light rake out, then come back to settle on Dicky's pack.

Somebody shouted from behind us. A couple of men yelled for us to stop, then there was a single shot that I took to be a warning. Dicky whispered back to me to follow him.

We crawled another few feet and the night erupted in gunfire. The flashing hurt my eyes, the reports stung my ears, and I nearly wet myself when I realized I was a target. The men on the ridge were firing down on us and the fire was being returned from the rear door and the broken stained-glass windows of the church.

"Hurry up! Hurry up!" voices shouted at us.

I rose to my feet and ran hunched over behind Dicky. I saw a tear form suddenly in his pack as a bullet penetrated it, and he fell, but he got up and kept moving and soon we were inside the building; the sound of the firefight had fallen to a shot every few seconds. I was panting and crawling across the planks until I was well into the middle of the floor, where I kicked my feet as if I were on fire or covered with spider webs. The room was lit by a couple of lanterns that shaded the room yellow and shook unreal shadows against the walls, reflecting brassy light off the shell casings by my feet. I looked around slowly, trying to believe it all, trying to see what there was to see, not believing for one second that I was really there. Tyrone Bisset was standing at the front window, looking out into the bright floods.

"I'm glad you could make it," he said without turning around to look at me.

All I could say was, "Oh, shit."

I slipped out of the pack and leaned my back against the leg of a table. "Tell me I'm not stuck here. Tell me I can walk out that door and go back to my house."

"I can't tell you that," he said.

Dicky had his pack open and was unloading it, and handing the goods to Louise and another woman I didn't know. The place smelled of sweat and wet wood and spent gunpowder. I watched Louise as she opened a large can of cling peaches, her little hands struggling with the can-opener blade of a Swiss Army knife. Beyond her, beyond the galley kitchen, I saw two men sitting on the floor. They were tied back-to-back and gagged; their ankles were bound and their feet bare. One of them was staring at me. Next to the hobbled men was a trunk, the old steamer kind like the one I took to college my first year.

"I've got to get out of here," I said.

"That's going to be tough," John Hat said, coming over and helping me to my feet and then into a ladder-back wooden chair. He sat beside me. "Scared?"

"No," I said.

"Me neither," he said.

"How did you end up with them?" I indicated the men who were tied up with a nod.

"They decided to chase us and got too close."

"Why were they chasing you?"

John Hat started to laugh. Tyrone Bisset was standing beside me now and he was laughing, too. "They were trying to get their leader back," Bisset said. "He's in the trunk."

"What are you talking about?"

"Custer," John Hat said. "We've got Custer in the trunk."

"How's he looking?" I asked.

Soon the whole room was busy with laughter, and now plates of food found laps, including mine. Louise handed me a cup of water as well and I studied her face.

"Are you all right?" I asked.

"Yes. What about you?"

"How's your mother?"

"She died."

I swallowed some of the water and took a bite of jerky.

. . .

. . . I have always felt, ever since I was a young officer in the Army, a great interest in the welfare of the Indians. I know that formerly they have been abused and their rights not properly respected. Since it has been in my power to have any control over Indian affairs I have endeavored to adopt a policy that should be for your future good, and calculated to preserve peace between whites and Indians for the present; and it is my great desire, now while I can retain some control over the matter, that the initiatory steps should be taken to secure you and your children hereafter. If you will cooperate with me I shall look always to what I believe is for your interests. Many of the Indians who accepted at an early day what we have proposed to you today are now living in

houses, have fences around their farms; *have school houses, and their children are reading and writing as we do here.*

. . .

My grandfather insisted that we split up. He told me that he would swing wide and come back over the dike and so flush any hiding animals out toward me. We'd never hunted that way before and I had a bad feeling about it.

"I think we should stay together," I said. "We've never split up before."

Grandfather was rubbing the barrel of his shotgun and then smelling the gun oil on his fingers. "We can't always be together, Grandson. This world is made to be felt alone. Everything important you do alone. Do you know what I mean? Even falling in love. And some things especially. So, I'll come up through the big laurels and you be ready, okay?"

. . .

Bisset was sitting in front of me, his braid coming undone over his shoulder. "Dicky tells me you saw the dump site."

"I took pictures of it." I said. "I guess he told you about the dam and the pipeline. I took pictures of those, too. A couple of rolls, actually. Above the dam is a clearing and it's not natural and it's melting snow like something's buried there."

"You're sure about the function of the dam?" he said.

"I know this drainage. The only reason can be to divert the runoff down into the Silly Man and so into the Plata. Right here." I pulled the canisters of film from my pocket and gave them to him. "I also marked the sites on my map."

Bisset grabbed my shoulder. "Thank you." He then walked over to the FBI hostages. "See this," he said to the them, holding the cans of film in front of their gagged faces. "Proof. Now maybe they'll listen."

Louise came over and touched my face, seeming smaller than ever, then she was at another table loading rifles.

. . .

I waited at the bend of the river. The bottom was quiet, the wind gently pushing through the boughs of the cypress trees. A flicker hammered briefly on a tree somewhere far off, and then its sound was swallowed by mist and drizzle. I recalled my grandfather's stride as we had gone in our separate directions: sure steps, as his steps used to be. The rain started to fall in earnest. I sat in there in the mud, waiting, crying.

. . .

In the morning, Bisset had written a letter of demands, including the fact that he now had something to substantiate their claims about the stored chemicals. One of the agents was untied—a short, fat man with a receding hairline—and Bisset gave him the letter, told him to take care of it, told him to remember his partner.

The FBI man looked around the room at all of us and then at his partner. "Your asses are cooked," he said.

"You'd better hope not," Bisset said.

John and Leonard Hat walked with the man through the front door. I moved to the window to watch. The man's naked feet looked so pink against the snow. The sky was so clear. The soldiers and cops stood in the distance, motionless, static as if they weren't quite real. Then something happened. A shot was fired from somewhere and then, just like the night before the air was full of bullets. Glass flew everywhere. Before I hit the floor I saw the unmoving game pieces across the flat lot and pasture move to take cover behind vehicles, bend to single knees, raise their weapons, and point them in our direction. When all was silent again and the air was again electric and thick with the pungent smell of gunfire, John and Leonard Hat lay dead on either side of the dead FBI man. Louise shoved a black and heavy rifle in my hands. Absently, I took it and sat on the bench near the rear wall. I could feel the oil of the weapon on my fingers and I raised them to my nose to smell it.

Colder air came through the window as darkness fell. Louise put some pieces of a broken chair into the woodstove and closed the doors. Bisset was sitting at the table, the yellow canisters of film in front of him. He was shaken by the loss of the Hat brothers. He looked over at the bound FBI agent and said, "I ought to just kill you right now. Even better, I ought to let you walk out that door so your own people will do it."

I couldn't take my eyes off the rolls of film and I kept feeling my grandfather, hearing his voice, remembering the sound of that report from his shotgun that rainy afternoon. I got up and walked to Bisset.

"Give me one of the rolls," I said.

Bisset looked at me. "What are you thinking?"

"I'm going to take a roll of film to the Naturalists' Conservancy office in Denver."

Louise stepped nearer along with a couple of the others to listen more closely.

"What, you think you're going to step out there and hitch a ride with a guardsman or something?" Bisset said.

"I know this mountain. I know this mountain better than anybody. They can't keep up with me."

Bisset shook his head. "You've got to get to it first."

"I can do that. When Dicky and I were crawling down the hill, we crossed an irrigation ditch."

"He's right," Dicky said.

"If I stay in the ditch, they'll never see me."

Bisset scratched his head. "Dicky, do you think you can make it like he says?"

"No," I said. "Dicky will only slow me down. He doesn't know the way and I can't spend time looking back for him. I have to do this alone. Sorry, Dicky."

Louise stepped around me to stand next to Bisset. "Why are you doing this?"

I laughed, more to myself than for them. "What else am I supposed to do?"

"I had you read all wrong," Louise said.

"No, you didn't," I said. I picked up a can of film, put it into the pocket of my vest, and zipped it shut. "I'll need the lights off so I can get out the back door."

"We can make a diversion for you," Dicky said.

"No," said Bisset. "That will only make the bastards more nervous and get them moving around."

I looked beyond Bisset and Louise out the window and saw snow falling through the darkness. "Good," I said. "The snow will help, give me a little more cover."

Bisset looked at my eyes. "I guess, I don't know what to say."

"Yeah, well, say it later," I told him. "Give me an Indian name or something like that when all this shit is over."

"You got it," Bisset said.

"But I don't want Dicky naming me."

Dicky laughed.

"Blow out the lanterns," Bisset said and the lights were put out. We stood around in the dark for a few minutes. Dicky asked me if I wanted a flashlight and I shoved it into my pocket, although I probably wouldn't be using it, since I planned to feel my way through the ditch to the Silly Man and up the mountain.

Bisset stood with me at the back door. "Thanks," he said and I nodded. He opened the door about eighteen inches and I crawled out into the snow.

The sky was deep gray and black and the snow was falling heavily now. I was too afraid to feel the cold. My gloved hands were searching the ground in front of me for the ditch. I was imagining crawling into the knees of one of the militia when I found the channel. I fell into it and made my way through it like a snake. Trying to think positively, I did acknowledge that to my good fortune there would be no snakes this time of year, but that sense of good fortune was quickly erased by the feeling of moisture seeping through the fabric of my gloves at my wrists and through the knees of my trousers. I wondered how long it would be before the symptoms of anthrax began to appear.

I stopped when I thought I heard footsteps. I waited until there was no sound. I didn't dare raise my head out of the ditch to look down the slope or up. I crawled again, my hands and knees now soaked, and then I was at the dirt-blocked source of the ditch and Silly Man Creek. I stayed low and made my way about a hundred yards up the creek along the bank, and then looked back to see that the church and all those stationed in front of it looked very far away. I took off my gloves and shoved them into a pocket. My hands were freezing and I put them under my coat to get them warm. I marched up the creek a couple of miles and finally felt safe enough to use the light Dicky had given me, but when I shone the beam into the darkness and falling snow I found it useless.

.   .   .

Article 4. To aid the said nations of Indians in their subsistence while removing to and making their settlement upon the said reservation, the United States will furnish them, free of charge, *with two thousand five hundred head of beef-cattle average in weight five hundred pounds,*

three hundred and fifty sacks of flour of one hundred pounds each,
within the term of two years from the date of this treaty.

. . .

I was stumbling by the time I knew I was near my cabin and the
snow had stopped falling. I approached the house slowly, my
hands aching, knowing I needed to thaw and dry before frostbite
set in. It was late morning when I walked in through the front
door, and there was Special Agent Davies, kneeling in front of the
stove, just getting ready to light a fire. I thought of running, but I
didn't. She looked at me and then lit the paper she had balled up
under the logs. I walked over to the stove and started peeling off
my wet clothes.

"So, here we are," she said.

"Here we are." I had my parka, vest, and shirt off and I was
loosening the laces of my boots. "So, what's the story? Are you
going to arrest me?" I asked.

"What did you do?"

"I must have done something." I kicked my boots off and removed my trousers.

"We never have been shy with each other," Davies said. She sat
in the big chair and stared at me.

I got close to the stove and tried to soak up the heat. "No Indians killed Begay and what's-his-name," I said. I grabbed my vest
from the floor and took the canister of film out of the pocket.

"What's that?"

"Proof of bad shit." Finally the fire was going strong and heat-
ing up the area around it. I began feel my fingers again. "I'm going
to get dressed and then I'm driving to Denver."

"Proof of what?"

"You'll see."

"Where were you?" she asked.

I realized that no one could prove where I had or had not been. "I was out hiking."

"Rough hike, I'd say from looking at you."

"Uphill both ways," I said, glancing at her. "Listen, I'm going to get dressed now."

"I'm not stopping you."

"You're not?" I asked.

She shook her head.

I studied her for a couple of seconds. "What are you saying? You mean, you're just going to let me drive out of here?"

"Is there some reason I should stop you?" She held me fast with her eyes and I could see that for the first time I was seeing her cold sober. She stood up and walked to the door, stopped and looked at me, but didn't say anything else before leaving.

The road was slick down to the junction, but there was little traffic. There were some men standing outside in front of Clara's store and they seemed anxious, agitated, and gave me hard stares as I rolled by. I had the heater blowing full, the hot air was cooking my legs, and the radio was switched to the all-news station, but all I heard were ball-game scores. I put my hand into the pocket of my jacket and felt the canister of film, which I rolled between my fingers. The sun came out and started melting the ice and snow on the highway.

I looked north at the mountain, jacketed in an overlay of snow. It looked so peaceful, so clean, so inert.

Acknowledgments

The Plata Reservation and the Plata Nation presented in this work are fictitious and are meant to bear no direct or indirect resemblance to any existing place or people. None of the characters are real, nor are they based in any way on existing individuals. The landscape of Plata Mountain is also complete fiction, including, and especially, the hydrologic data presented.

The excerpts from treaties between the United States government and various Indian nations used in this novel are a matter of public record, but I would like to acknowledge as a valuable source *Indian Treaties 1778–1883,* compiled and edited by Charles Kappler (Amereon House, Mattituck, NY, 1972). I would also like to thank Ward Churchill and Jim Vander Wall, authors of *Agents of Repression: The FBI's Secret Wars Against the Black Panther Party and the American Indian Movement* (South End Press, Boston, MA, 1988) for sending me to some documents I found helpful.